Dr. Nightingale Races the Outlaw Colt

A DEIRDRE QUINN NIGHTINGALE MYSTERY

Lydia Adamson

A SIGNET BOOK

SIGNET
Published by the Penguin Group
Penguin Putnam Inc., 375 Hudson Street,
New York, New York 10014, U.S.A.
Penguin Books Ltd, 27 Wrights Lane,
London W8 5TZ, England
Penguin Books Australia Ltd,
Ringwood, Victoria, Australia
Penguin Books Canada Ltd, 10 Alcorn Avenue,
Toronto, Ontario, Canada M4V 3B2
Penguin Books (N.Z.) Ltd, 182–190 Wairau Road,
Auckland 10, New Zealand

Penguin Books Ltd, Registered Offices:
Harmondsworth, Middlesex, England

First published by Signet, an imprint of Dutton Signet,
a member of Penguin Putnam Inc.

First Printing, February, 1998
10 9 8 7 6 5 4 3 2 1

Chapter 1

Deirdre Quinn Nightingale, Doctor of Veterinary Medicine, was just about to climb into the tub when her elderly veterinary assistant, Charlie Gravis, knocked at the bedroom door.

Her clothes for the evening were already laid out on the bed. And rather fancy clothes they were for a weeknight dinner in Hillsbrook. But she was going to the fanciest restaurant in town—a new place, called Artichoke. Allie Voegler was taking her, along with Wynton Chung.

It was a celebratory dinner, in honor of Chung's second year with the Hillsbrook Police Department; a private celebration, just the three of them.

Allie had been on the force eight years and was the department's only plainclothes detective. He considered Chung his protégé. And he considered Didi his wife, although this was more wish than fact. They were simply lovers.

Didi put on a bathrobe and opened the door. The old man was puffing from climbing the stairs.

"We just got a call," he said.

"From who?"

"Aden Fox. He says he needs you fast. He says three of his milk cows are in bad trouble."

There was no hesitation on Didi's part. The clients and their beasts came first.

"Get the Jeep ready, Charlie!" She glanced at the dark silk dress on the bed. Well, she thought, I can do what has to be done at the Fox farm, then run back home to shower and change, and then go to the restaurant.

She hurriedly put her work clothes back on, then called the Artichoke and left a message for Allie that she'd be a bit late.

As the red Jeep headed toward the Fox property, Didi felt that rush of adrenaline. If she ever had doubts about the veterinary profession, those doubts were always swept away on an emergency call.

Allie had once told her: "I believe in my heart that if you had the choice between saving a sick sow and a sick me, the pig would win—hands down."

She laughed out loud at the memory.

Charlie, in the passenger seat, demanded, "What's so funny?"

He was grumpy. He didn't like emergency calls—especially after hours. And he didn't like the idea that she had neglected to put up the canvas sides of the vehicle. The wind was buffeting him about as they drove.

"Oh, nothing," Didi said. "Nothing at all's funny."

It was almost dark when they reached the Fox place. Aden Fox was waiting for them in front of the lighted barn.

"Good to see you again," Charlie muttered.

Aden just nodded. He looked troubled, nervous, pulling at his crisscrossed suspenders. He was a young man, very thin, with a shock of brown hair falling down into his eyes. His father had owned and worked the farm before him. A baby was crying in the nearby house.

Fox led them into the barn. "Three of them," he said to Didi. "In stalls five, eight, and ten. The others are fine."

She walked to stall number five, unbuttoning her short denim jacket. Charlie and Aden followed close behind.

She studied the cow. It was a sorry sight. The animal was standing stiffly with head lowered, breathing heavily through an open mouth.

The rasping sounds from her chest indicated some kind of emphysema or edema-type lesions on the lungs.

The cow remained absolutely still, not making even the slightest movement of its head.

"The other two are exactly like this. They came down with it suddenly. I got them in from the pasture only three hours ago."

Aden Fox's voice began to crack.

Charlie whispered to Didi, "I've been mucking

out dairy barns a whole bunch of years, and I never saw a cow stand like that."

Didi raised her hand in a gesture to indicate that he should be quiet.

She had in fact seen something like this condition before.

But not in real life. She'd seen it in a film shown at a veterinary workshop she had attended two years ago in Washington, D.C. Sponsored by the U.S.D.A., the title of the workshop was "Poisonous Plants of Temperate North America." The emphasis was on recently "escaped" plants.

Didi moved halfway into the stall.

A pungent odor was rising from the stall straw, which was soaked with urine.

It was a very strange smell—almost like a sweet and sour horseradish.

"Aren't you going to examine her?" Aden asked impatiently.

Didi ignored his question and asked one of her own: "Where were they grazing today?"

"In the south pasture."

"High grass?"

"This time of year? You must be kidding. Mostly close-cropped patches."

"Wet?"

"Dry as a bone."

"You have a large-beam torch, Aden?"

"Sure," he said, pointing at an equipment wall between two stalls. "But what the hell does this have to do with the price of tea?"

Again, she did not answer him. She saw the huge flashlight. She walked over and pulled it off the hook.

"Who owns the adjoining property, Aden?"

"It's the Stringfellow place."

"Any pastures?"

"No. It's just a swampy, overgrown field. They don't farm over there. They use the house only for summers. Anyway, my place is fenced all around."

Didi marched out of the barn, signaling that they should follow.

"Where are we going?" Aden demanded angrily.

"Why don't you just do what the doc tells you to do?" Charlie rebuked him. "She's the best damn vet in Dutchess County."

The trio headed toward the road, Didi in the lead.

Charlie kept after the young farmer. "She may look like a kid, but don't let that pretty face fool you. She knows more about cows than you, your father, and me put together."

When she reached the beginning of the high, three-rail wood fence, she began to follow it along the perimeter of the pasture.

About two hundred yards in, Didi stopped short and raised the beam high.

Charlie whistled and said, "Would you take a look at that!"

All the rails in a five- or six-foot span had been smashed. One could drive a small truck through.

"My cows wouldn't do that," Aden said, confused.

"I believe you," Didi replied. "Cows don't kick this way. Look at the top rail—at the pieces of splintered wood. It was broken from the top down. From a rearing animal—up on the hind legs and down onto the wood. Maybe a deer. Maybe a horse."

Didi walked through the gap in the fence, onto marshy ground. Her beam was now focused low and she was bent over.

They had walked only about twenty feet when Didi let out an exuberant "Yes!"

She squatted on the ground, and Charlie and Fox peered over her shoulder.

"Here it is," she said.

The beam was shining on several small shrubs. They had branched, squared stems. The serrated leaves were purplish. A few still had small white flowers.

Didi broke off a stalk, stood up, and thrust it at Aden Fox.

"Take a whiff, Aden."

He did, and understood at once. "The same smell as in the stalls," he said.

"Right. I don't know the technical name of the plant. But the common names are Perilla Mint and Beefsteak Plant. It's an ornamental indigenous to India. Somehow it 'escaped' to this country. Cattle love it. But in summer and fall, it's poison."

"So what do we do now?" Aden pressed.

Didi gave Charlie a quick glance. The old dairy farmer knew what it meant: very little could be done.

"I'll tell it to you straight, Aden. First of all, you're lucky. Only three of your cows seem to have eaten the plant. But we can't be sure. It usually takes two to ten days for symptoms to appear. Your cows came down with them in a few hours. This may be good news or bad news. Frankly, I don't know."

She paused. She flicked the beam on and off in the darkness. A wind had come up and was whipping all around them.

"You have to do something for them," Aden pleaded.

"I will. But medication only works, if it works at all, on cows still symptom-free. The three cows already sick may or may not recover on their own. Charlie and I will treat the rest of the herd. Half on steroids and antibiotics. Half on antihistamines and antibiotics."

They headed back through the shattered fence toward the barn.

Didi arrived at the restaurant ninety minutes late, still in her rank and muddy work clothes.

It was a lovely place, a converted farmhouse. The front bar was packed, but in the dining area only three tables were occupied.

"The hostess thought I was a madwoman," Didi

said, laughing, as she sat down. "I must smell like thirty milk cows from hell."

"You smell beautiful! You look beautiful! You are beautiful!" Allie shouted. Then he reached over and ran his hand through her short black hair.

Didi was startled. Allie seldom indulged in such public outbursts of affection. In his good suit and tie, he looked like a burly boy home from school for the holidays.

In contrast, Wynton Chung, who considered himself urbane, wore a black turtleneck and plain light-colored trousers.

"There was some trouble at Aden Fox's farm," Didi told them.

Allie filled her glass with champagne, then re-filled his and Chung's. "I wish to make a toast," he said.

They raised their glasses.

"To every living creature on Aden Fox's farm," Allie said, his voice full of emotion.

They all drank. It was obvious to Didi what these two had been doing while waiting for her. What else is new? she thought.

She called for a menu then. Oh, this was a treat! She loved French cuisine but rarely had the chance to partake of it.

"We kept ordering appetizers," Allie boasted, "and now we're both stuffed. But you have not yet begun to eat, Doctor Nightingale."

She ordered pâté, a small salad, and a duck dish she couldn't pronounce.

The food came quickly and she devoured it, course by course. Allie kept refilling her glass.

I am getting tipsy also, she thought. But she didn't much mind. She needed something so as not to think about the dice game being played out in the Fox barn. She needed bubbly to get that pungent, poisonous stench out of her nostrils.

When the unpronounceable main dish was bones, she asked for coffee and a luscious fruit tart with whipped cream. Allie and Wynton Chung had about exhausted their conversation with each other. They were watching Didi eat.

Halfway through dessert, she sat back and said, "I surrender."

Allie applauded. "You did good, Dr. Nightingale. Cow trouble put an edge on your appetite."

Didi closed her eyes. She felt good, full, calm, at ease. Her thoughts went to Aden and she felt a twinge of guilt at being in this sumptuous restaurant while he sat at home worrying. She knew dairy farmers. He would remain in the barn all night—waiting, hoping.

"Do you hear music?" Wynton Chung asked.

Didi opened her eyes.

Yes. She heard it. Someone was playing "The Nearness of You" on the piano. Old-fashioned song. Old-fashioned love. It made her feel even better.

"Where's it coming from?" she asked.

"After ten, they bring in a piano player to the bar," Allie explained. "They even clear an area for slow dancing." He found that funny. So did Chung. Didi couldn't find the joke, if there was one.

"I'd like to dance," she said.

Allie paid the bill and the three of them repaired to the front of the restaurant.

There were ten or twelve people lined up at the bar, but she didn't recognize any of them from Hillsbrook. The pianist was a thin black woman wearing a very tight-fitting dress with a lovely purple scarf around her neck.

They ordered more champagne and went on making sillier and sillier toasts to each other, or to no one at all.

"I think I should get the first dance," Allie said.

"By all means," Didi agreed.

They walked out to the makeshift dance floor, which was simply a cleared space between cocktail tables.

The music was slow and lovely. Allie was light on his feet for a large man. She felt glorious. Oh! It had been a long time since she danced like this—to this kind of music. It was the way her mother used to dance with the mop while she cleaned—the radio on—just a simple two-step; once in a while a little break or dip.

Then the pianist picked up the beat a bit—some "Buttermilk Sky" and other Hoagy Carmichael songs.

"Why don't you let a pro take over?" a voice

said behind them. It was Wynton Chung. Allie handed her over.

Didi was astonished at how fine a dancer the young police officer was. Almost like a dance instructor, leading her gently into intricate breaks.

She found herself getting more and more into the spirit of it.

"You're good!" she said breathlessly.

"When you've got a Chinese father and a black mom, you have to be good," he replied.

Other dancers were on the floor now. The piano player went into a rhumba. Didi had no idea how to rhumba. She had only seen it done in the old movies. But Wynton Chung knew how. He led her easily into the steps, using his hands to show her which way to move.

She began to feel a bit wild. She threw herself into the dance.

But then her head began to ache. And the smoke from the cigarettes at the bar began to make her eyes tear.

She saw that someone had opened the front door of the restaurant, leaving only the screen door shut.

"Why don't we dance outside?" Didi suggested.

"Good idea," Chung said.

She took him by the hand and led him back to the bar where Allie sat with his drink.

"We're going outside," she said. "Come with us. We can hear the music through the screen door—and I can breathe."

"But it's the parking lot! How can you dance in a parking lot?"

Didi laughed, leaned over, and kissed him.

"I can dance anywhere."

He pulled away from her. "No! That's stupid. You're drunk, Didi."

Her angry reaction was instantaneous. "Why do you always give orders? Sooner or later you always start playing the big bad cop. Don't play that game with me!"

Still holding Wynton's hand, she pulled him away. They pushed the screen door open and walked out onto the small parking lot.

"I hear the music fine out here," Didi said triumphantly.

Just as they were about to reconstitute their rhumba routine, a car in the parking lot turned on its brights.

"Shut them off!" Didi shouted, half blinded by the sudden light.

The driver complied, but not before a weapon in the driver's hand, thrust out the window, spat out three bullets that tore into Wynton Chung's chest.

As he fell, he convulsively pulled Didi down with him. She landed heavily on the body.

How long did she lay there? She didn't know.

Then rough hands were pulling her away. It was Allie. He bent over Chung. He was yelling to someone to call an ambulance.

She watched in a daze. She saw him trying to breathe life into Wynton Chung's chest.

She heard him begging Chung to blink his eyes.

Then he sat back on his haunches and began to rock, the tears streaming down his face.

"I told you not to go outside," he kept saying in a kind of intonation.

Didi could think of nothing to say in answer.

Chapter 2

A cool morning wind came out of the west and made the kitchen panes shudder.

"Will you look at that!" Mrs. Tunney said. "Have you ever seen anything so sad?"

Dr. Nightingale's elves crowded behind the matronly Mrs. Tunney: Trent Tucker, the young handyman, was sipping his coffee as he stared out the window. Charlie Gravis had his fingers hooked over his belt buckle. The keeper of the yard dogs and groom for Dr. Nightingale's horse, Promise Me—the strange young girl called Abigail—moved off to one side, as if looking might be painful. Her long golden hair was done in two braids. Her lovely face was, as usual, a blank.

"What the hell is she doing?" Charlie asked.

They were all staring at Dr. Deirdre Quinn Nightingale, who was seated lotus position on the ground as she sat every morning. But this time it was different. She obviously wasn't performing her usual yogic breathing exercises.

No. She appeared instead to be brooding, perhaps even weeping—her head hanging down limply on her chest.

"She's not going to the funeral," Charlie said.

Mrs. Tunney, who had her large oatmeal spoon in her right hand, raised it menacingly to the window. "If that Voegler fellow was here, I would smash him right between the eyes . . . police officer or not!"

Even Charlie Gravis was astonished by her vehemence.

"What did he do?" Trent Tucker asked. And then added, "I mean, he didn't kill Wynton Chung."

"What do you mean, what did he do? Don't you have eyes and ears? She's been moping around since that terrible thing happened. And it's Voegler's fault. He doesn't answer her calls, he doesn't come to see her. He doesn't do anything but avoid her. Because he's an idiot."

"Well," said Charlie philosophically, "you never liked him."

"It'll all blow over," Trent Tucker said.

"I think it's over now," said Mrs. Tunney. "I mean really over. And good riddance to bad rubbish."

Mrs. Tunney smacked the spoon down to underscore her point.

Trent Tucker looked at Abigail for support. Mrs. Tunney had, as usual, misunderstood him. Abigail made no gesture of support. He plunged ahead.

"From what I hear around, he told the doc not to go out into the parking lot to dance with Chung.

But she wouldn't listen. She went out there. And boom! One dead cop."

In the yard Didi raised her head. The elves scrambled away from the window. They sat down at the table. Mrs. Tunney brought the blue-and-white oatmeal tureen. Butter, sugar, cream, and toast were already in place.

"The way I look at it . . ." Charlie began, but then he paused. Everyone seemed to be waiting for some words of wisdom from the old man. After all, Charlie worked closely with Dr. Nightingale. He made rounds with her. But for some reason, he wasn't capable of finishing whatever thought he had, so everyone turned from him and attacked the oatmeal.

Except for Mrs. Tunney. It was obvious she was still too upset to eat.

Abigail buttered a piece of toast slowly, fastidiously, and then spoke her first words of the morning. "Miss Quinn (most of the elves called Didi that out of respect for her late mother, who had taken them all in) told me that marriage is a distinct possibility."

"God forbid!" Mrs. Tunney exclaimed. Then she cautioned Charlie with a gesture against his excessive use of brown sugar in his oatmeal. He ignored her and stirred in several heaping tablespoons full.

"I used to really hate Allie Voegler," Trent Tucker confessed. "He was always hassling me and my friends. But now I don't think he's such a bad guy."

"Bad *guy*? What does that mean? A good *man* doesn't make his lady friend unhappy," Mrs. Tunney retorted. "And believe me, poor Miss Quinn is a very unhappy miss. I have never seen her so sad. Just sitting out there at six in the morning—brooding, a minute away from tears. Just sitting there! Can you imagine it!"

Charlie nodded in approval at her exposition; then he stared with contempt at Trent Tucker, who was shaking salt on his oatmeal. Charlie could never understand people who put salt on oatmeal; it was just plain crazy.

"Why don't you try some pepper also?" he shot over to Trent. Abigail giggled. Trent ignored the old coot.

When they heard the back door open, they all fell silent and sat up stiffly in their chairs.

"Good morning," Didi said in a barely audible voice. She walked to the stove and poured herself some coffee in a large chipped cup. Without another word she walked down the hallway that led to the stairs and her bedroom.

"Oh, this is terrible," Mrs. Tunney whispered. "Did you ever see her so bad off?"

"Look at it this way," Charlie consoled her, "two out of three of Aden Fox's cows recovered. And the rest of his herd never got sick. Think how sad she would be if the veterinary news was bad too."

For some reason, Mrs. Tunney didn't find this consoling at all.

* * *

The service was held in a small Roman Catholic church in Kingston. The burial was in a cemetery just north of the town. Allie had no idea that Wynton Chung had been a Catholic. Religion had never been discussed. They had talked about all kinds of things in their careless bantering style, but never that.

The Hillsbrook Police Department supplied the pallbearers and Allie was one of them.

When the coffin emerged from the church, all Allie could see was blue. Virtually every police department in Dutchess County had sent an official contingent—resplendent in their dress uniforms.

As the casket moved down the steps toward the waiting hearse, Allie found the whole spectacle repugnant. Chung was no hero cop. He might have become one had he lived, but he had been ambushed and assassinated like a feral dog that runs deer. Before his time—way before his time. Besides, Wynton Chung prided himself on being hip . . . on being cool. He would have laughed at a gung ho funeral, at the military model so dear to police departments.

The pallbearers paused at the bottom of the church steps. The father, John Chung, and the brother in from California, Darryl Chung, walked past—stiff and dazed.

Allie had met the father once before, briefly. Father and son had not gotten along very well. Chung Senior was a professor of history at the State University at New Paltz. And he had been very unhappy with his younger son's choice of profession. The mother, Allie knew, was long dead. Darryl Chung was a chemist for a drug company in San Francisco. Wynton had rarely spoken about him.

The moment the casket reached graveside Allie began to crumble. It happened in stages. First, he had the feeling that the body in the casket was not Wynton Chung. Then, even though he was wearing his uniform, and even though he had a sweater under the outfit to ward off the morning chill, at the moment it occurred to him that Chung was not inside that box, he began to shake uncontrollably. Then he was hit with a wave of bitterness and guilt so ferocious that he could barely stand erect. Tiny beads of cold sweat covered his face and neck.

He could see the scene unrolling again and again. Like a home movie of death: Didi walking out with Wynton Chung—or dancing out. He could hear his own words telling her not to go. Had he known what was about to happen? Had he intuited it? Oh, that stubborn, stubborn woman!

Then Allie Voegler just imploded, and stood dumbly, hearing nothing, seeing nothing.

When the funeral was completed, he did not go to a bar with the Hillsbrook contingent. He drove slowly back home and parked in front of a small, tacky motel near the Agway market.

In Wynton Chung's two years on the force, he had lived in three places. This one, the Whitetail Inn, had been the last. It had once been a favorite of deer hunters in the fall and antique hunters in the spring. But now it was hopelessly run-down. Chung had told Allie, "They rent rooms by the hour now. Wham, bam, thank you, ma'am. Little do they know, there's a cop in the next room doing the crossword puzzle. It amuses me, Allie."

Voegler just sat at the wheel. The sun was coming fiercely through the windshield.

I have to go in there, he thought. I have to slowly and meticulously go through Chung's room. Dismantle it. I have to take it apart sock by sock.

He reached into his pocket, pulled out a pack of Newports, and smoked the first cigarette he had had in six years.

He uprooted all the poisonous shrubs just over the fence line and put them in a large black plastic garbage bag. These would be burned.

One of the shrubs he carefully put aside and brushed the dirt off the roots. This one he put into a smaller, blue plastic bag. She would send it, he knew, to a USDA lab in Maryland. Why, he wondered, are there so many damn labs in Maryland? Don't they fish there anymore?

Then Charlie Gravis straightened up slowly. His back hurt. He was too old for this kind of work. He leaned on the splintered fence. Aden Fox had not fixed it yet—not properly, anyway. He had merely nailed two boards crisscross over the gap.

Charlie could see that Dr. Nightingale and the dairy farmer had come out of the barn and were chatting. Or rather, Aden was talking a mile a minute while Didi just stood listening. He's probably making a fool of himself, Charlie thought, thanking the vet as if her ministrations had saved his herd. Luck, Charlie knew, saved those cows. Old Lady Luck.

Then the young vet and the dairy farmer shook hands and Didi headed for the fence.

"I'm all done here," Charlie announced as soon as she got close. He pointed to the bags as evidence of the completion of his job. She nodded, but when she reached the fence she peered over and scrutinized the ground to make sure he had not missed any of the small shrubs. Charlie was a little annoyed, but all he did was scowl.

"I'm going over to Rose Vigdor's place," Didi said. "You take the Jeep back. Rose will give me a lift home later on."

Charlie nodded, picked up the bags, and headed toward the road on one side of the fence; Didi walked along the other side.

Twenty yards from the road, Charlie had an uncanny sense that they were not alone, as if someone were watching them. He felt it strongly. He stopped, ostensibly to rest, and put the bags down.

"Do you need a hand?" Didi asked him.

The vet and her associate saw the couple then, standing on the cinder path that led to the Stringfellow house—the property on which Charlie was in essence trespassing.

The man and woman stood absolutely still. They

were holding hands. Both were tall, middle-aged, and city dressed, and both were openly staring.

"Hello," Didi called to the two and waved. Then, turning to Charlie, she said, "I thought they were only here in the summer. That's what Aden Fox told us."

"You think they're the Stringfellows?"

"I guess they are."

Neither Ruth nor Walter Stringfellow responded to Didi's greeting.

"Not too chatty, those two," Charlie noted rue-fully. "At least they don't seem to be mad at us for digging up their shrubbery."

"They don't even seem curious," Didi added.

"They stand there like they're posing for a pic-ture," he said. "Most couples that age don't hold hands."

Then the two strangers began to walk toward their house. They had left a large blue Volvo at the foot of the path. Didi waved to them again. Again they ignored her, so she and Charlie continued their journey to the red Jeep.

Ten minutes later, Charlie dropped her at Rose Vigdor's place. He then drove to the Hillsbrook Diner where he would have coffee. The parking lot was full up, so he had to station the Jeep on the side of the road, just north of the diner.

As he was climbing down from the vehicle he saw a flash of movement on the slope that rose from the road to a tree-lined ridge.

At first he thought it was a deer. But when he

had both feet on the ground he realized a woman was standing halfway up the slope.

She was wearing a yellow rain slicker and a matching hat. But it wasn't raining. She was staring down at the ground.

"Is everything okay?" Charlie called out, ever the gentleman. He had never seen the woman before. But then again, he had never seen that Stringfellow couple before either. As he got older, he knew fewer and fewer people in Hillsbrook. Sometimes it seemed that he was waking up in a strange town every morning.

The woman did not look up.

He needed some coffee but—well, something was out of whack. What was she doing up there? What could she be staring at on a roadside slope? A dead skunk?

"Hello, miss! Hey up there!"

She looked at him calmly, a kind and knowing smile on her face.

"Are you okay?" Charlie shouted.

"Oh, I'm much more than okay," she answered.

"What?"

"Come on up here and see!" she said brightly. It was neither a plea nor an order. Her voice remained low and friendly.

Charlie labored up the slope. When he was at last face to face with the woman, she took off her hat. He was startled at how close cropped her hair was. She looked to be about fifty, with a wide, friendly face that showed a wrinkle here and there.

She was broad shouldered and no more than five feet high.

Charlie was still puffing from the trek up.

"Look!" She pointed to the ground.

All he could see was a little clump of tiny umbrella mushrooms among the brown weeds. They were ubiquitous in the Hillsbrook area.

"Do you see them?"

"You mean those mushrooms?"

"Yes."

"I see 'em. What about them?"

"Don't you understand? They could have arisen anywhere."

"What are you talking about, miss?"

"Randomness, that's what. It's random—understand? They're here at our feet. But they could just as well be across the road. It's the spores. They propagate by spores."

She seemed calm, but her voice was clearly conveying her excitement. Charlie regarded her in perplexity.

"Don't you understand? There is nothing more random in the world than where a mushroom will pop up. The spores float across the world. Where they land—they land. No rhyme. No reason. Sheer, total, radical randomness! Truly written on the wind."

He had no idea what she was talking about, yet there was something charming about the way she spoke . . . so charming and heartfelt, in fact, that he had a sudden furious desire to kiss her.

The realization flustered him so much that he quickly nodded good-bye, rushed down the slope, and gained refuge in the diner, where he ordered a large coffee.

Dr. Nightingale finished her story lying on the dirt floor of her friend Rose's "converted" barn. Actually it was anything but converted. It was a primitive living space for a young refugee from urban life with three dogs and the vague belief that she was some kind of Lady Thoreau.

The heating and electrical systems that Rose had told Didi she was finally installing somehow never appeared. But Didi, lying there on the worn rattan rug, was quite content. It was the first time since the tragedy that she had spoken more than a couple of words to anyone.

"That is the strangest story I've ever heard," said Rose. "I mean, does that idiot really believe you purposely led Chung to his death? That you set him up by dancing him out the door so somebody could kill him?"

"I don't know what he believes," Didi replied morosely and then had to cover her head as two of Rose's dogs—the corgi Huck and the young shepherd Bozo—ran over her as they chased each other. The third dog, the matronly shepherd bitch Aretha, looked on disapprovingly.

"Were you getting along before this happened?" Rose asked. "Was there a fight? Had the sex gone bad?"

Didi did not answer directly. She thought it over. It would be hard to characterize her affair with Allie Voegler as the great love of her life. It wasn't that by any stretch of the imagination. But she had been content. After all, she had been alone a long time. As for him, she knew he loved her deeply. Yes, she knew that, and it often made her uncomfortable.

"No," Didi finally said. "Everything was going along fine."

"Fine? I always get nervous when I hear that word," Rose mused.

Didi laughed. It was good to laugh again. Suddenly Aretha growled. A low, fierce sound.

"What's the matter with you now?" Rose challenged the shepherd bitch who, though still lying down, was now baring her teeth.

"She really loves me," a voice called out from the area of the barn door.

Rose and Didi were startled by the intruder's voice. Neither of them had heard the car drive up.

"My God! Speak of the devil!" Rose exclaimed. "It's Allie. I never saw you in uniform before. I didn't know detectives had uniforms."

Allie moved closer, two small plastic bags in hand. Didi didn't say a word. Aretha calmed down.

"Have you two ever met?" Rose asked jokingly. "Let me introduce you."

Allie addressed Didi. "I didn't know you'd be here."

"Ah," Rose said, "then you've come to arrest me." She thrust her wrists forward as if for the handcuffs to be attached.

Allie slapped the two packages he was carrying into her outstretched hands so suddenly that she staggered backward.

"They're yours, aren't they?" he said calmly.

"Mine?" asked Rose.

"Yeah. Yours. Does anybody else eat white cheddar cheese and spinach chips? I found them in Chung's room at the motel. You went to see him there, didn't you?"

Didi looked on, speechless and confused. Rose had turned pale.

Allie turned on Didi with a fury then. "Why didn't you tell me they were lovers?"

She said nothing.

"Are you her shrink as well as her friend?" he shouted. "Is that it? Some kind of doctor-patient privilege has kicked in here? Or maybe you're her priest. Is that it? The integrity of the Confessional?"

Rose dropped the bags to the floor. The dogs rushed over to them.

"Leave her alone, Allie," Rose said. "I never told Didi a thing about Wynton Chung and me. She didn't know."

Dr. Nightingale walked slowly over to Rose and kissed her on the cheek. "I'm walking home, Rose. I'll speak to you later."

As she passed Allie, she stopped. Not looking at

him she said, "You haven't been answering my calls. But there won't be any more. No calls. No conversations. No anything. We're through. Do you understand that, you stupid man?"

She buttoned the top of her denim work jacket and walked out.

Chapter 3

Detective Albert Voegler, the only plainclothes officer on the Hillsbrook Police Department, was back in his working garb and drinking a beer at Jacks, a bar he never frequented socially.

Jacks was where the kids in Hillsbrook drank: the out-of-work twenty-three-year-olds; the younger hot-rodders; the potheads, the just-discharged marines and sailors wondering whether to reenlist, because they had nothing better to do with their lives.

It was where one of Dr. Nightingale's elves, Trent Tucker, hung out.

No one at Jacks liked Allie Voegler—except maybe the bartender. But that was just fine by Allie. He wanted to be left alone. He had to think. He had to have a few drinks so that he felt calm enough and clear-headed enough to do some hard work.

Allie knew that since the murder of Chung he had been a loose cannon. But what else could be expected? The Chung case was as cold as a Milky

Way at the South Pole. No one knew a damn thing. The bullet had shattered upon impact, so the only thing ballistics could tell him was that probably— and they emphasized *probably*—it had come from a standard caliber deer rifle. And wasn't that helpful! There were probably 100,000 such rifles in Dutchess County alone.

Even worse was the fact that no one at the restaurant that night could identify the car in the parking lot from which the round was fired. No one had seen anything. Not even the car model or color. Not even a partial plate. And no one had seen a man or a woman waiting in a vehicle or in the back of a pickup truck at the time of the shooting. Nor had anyone been spotted coming in or out of the lot after the shooting. And no one had seen the fleeing vehicle.

Allie upended the beer bottle and took a very long swig. He put the bottle down, lit a Newport, and pulled a sheet of computer paper from his pants pocket, unrolling it on the bar like a scroll.

He took another swig of beer, finished the bottle, ordered another, and swiveled on the stool to check out the clientele. At this time of the afternoon, Jacks was almost empty. Two young men at a booth sat smoking, drinking beer, talking in low tones, as if what they had to say was conspiratorial and important. Ah, he thought, the delusions of kids.

He tried to remember the bar he used to sneak into as a high school student, all those years ago. It wasn't this joint. It was a joint in a trailer that sat in an old cow pasture south of the town. Bottles of Bud and packs of Marlboros. And "grass" sold out back of the place, if you had the price.

One thing was sure—Deirdre Quinn Nightingale never went in there with him. In high school she had scorned him, written him off as just another bumpkin macho biker. As she did now . . . as she surely did now.

He winced just thinking how stupidly he had acted. He could not believe that he had lost so quickly and totally the thing—the person—he treasured most in this world.

Maybe all this craziness would pass quickly. Maybe he would find the animal who had murdered Chung. And then—maybe—he would get back the woman he loved. And they would be married. Yes, they'd get married and he would leave the department and become a country gentleman and raise organic goats.

He started laughing so uncontrollably at the country gentleman idea that the bartender gave him a concerned look.

Allie shook off his mirth, bitter as it was, and smoothed out the printout. It was a computer-generated record of all individuals who left the state prison jurisdiction during June, July, and August of the current year, either via parole, completion of sentence, or judicial overturning of conviction.

The list was alphabetical by convict's last name,

annotated with the last facility of incarceration, type of conviction, and an indication whether departure was through parole or release.

Voegler had asked for the list on the morning after a sleepless night in which he realized the obvious: Wynton Chung had been murdered out of revenge . . . payback. And since Chung was clean as a whistle, it had to be someone he had hurt bad during his two years as a Hillsbrook officer.

It had to be someone he collared and convicted.

That was why Allie was methodically checking and cross-checking, scratching names off that long, sad list.

Now, in Jacks, he had to remember. Case files were worthless. Written-up cases are gobbledygook. No—his memory was better.

He took a small sip of beer and ran his finger down the names until he came to Lawrence Eisle, paroled after serving nineteen months on a three-year sentence for B&E. He had done his time in Otisville—not a nice place.

Yes, Eisle had been Chung's first collar. It had become a department legend because of the circumstances leading up to said collar. Rookie Chung was returning to headquarters after completing his uniformed patrol. It was nearly two in the morning. Suddenly he had to answer the call of nature. He pulls the car off the road and walks into a clump of trees. As he is urinating, he sees a large house past the trees. The place is dark. Then he

sees a pickup, lights dimmed, pulling up in front
of the house. A young man climbs out, smashes a
window, unlocks it from inside, opens the front
door, and proceeds to loot the house, oblivious to
the cop in the grove.

Chung buttons up his fly, waits a few minutes,
then arrests one Lawrence Eisle.

It was a bittersweet memory for Allie. He fiddled with the beer bottle, lit another cigarette. He
could not recall what Eisle looked like.

He moved down the page to the next name he
had marked with an asterisk: Sherman Porter.

This one's face he remembered. Porter was an
old man, skinny. Allie remembered the details of
the case as Chung had recounted them to him over
coffee and donuts. One thing about that kid
Chung—he loved donuts.

"Poor old bastard." That was how Chung had
characterized Porter, a bankrupt dairy farmer. He
had decided to survive by fleecing elderly widows of dairy farmers in a three-county area. The
scam was nutty but it worked on gullible, frightened, sometimes senile old women. Give Porter
$7,500 and he would obtain pensions for the
widow from the federal government. The money
is just waiting for her in a "special program" that
was set up in 1949 but never publicized. It will
pay her $1,200 a month for the remainder of the
widow's life.

One of the fleeced women contacted Chung. He

went after Porter and got him on a lesser charge—mail fraud.

Allie folded the paper. He took a long swallow of his beer and leaned back to listen to the music. But the music had stopped. Neither Eisle nor Porter had the profile of a cold-blooded payback cop killer, he knew. He laughed suddenly at his display of logic, after the fact. Chung was gone. Obliterated. It was as if he never was.

Allie lay his head on the bar and closed his eyes. He had never felt so tired in his life.

It was growing dark. Trent Tucker's beat-up truck was bouncing home on bad shock absorbers. Charlie Gravis sat quietly beside the young driver, the bags of groceries between his legs.

"What's the matter with you, Charlie? You haven't said a word in hours."

Charlie waved the question away with a hand. He had nothing to say to this young fool. Besides, he couldn't answer the question intelligently.

For two days, ever since meeting that strange woman on the slope, among the mushrooms, he had been in a terrible state, boiling over with something he hadn't experienced in a long time: sexual desire. Love . . . passion . . . and whatever else it could be called. Damn! He was seventy-two years old. Tired. As beat-up as Trent's old truck. Dead-ended. Broke. It was all just too much.

"In fact," the younger man went on, "even Abigail says you're acting kind of funny."

"Why don't you shut up and drive, you—"

Charlie never finished that nasty response. He had seen a figure on the far side of the road, someone with a walking stick.

At first, just for a moment, he thought it was the town poet, that crazy Bert Conyers, who often walked the roads with his homemade staff.

But no. It was a woman. A woman in yellow raingear.

"Stop!"

Trent Tucker looked over at the old man in alarm. "What is it?"

"I said stop the goddamn truck—now!"

Tucker braked. The pickup shuddered to a halt. Charlie scrambled out and ran across the road.

"Hey!" he began to yell.

The lady kept walking. And Charlie kept following her, calling as he ran, "Miss! Miss! Wait!"

Her pace never slowed. Was she deaf or something? Well, no, that couldn't be it. She seemed to have heard and spoken normally that day in the mushroom patch. Finally, he caught up to her, and pulled at her sleeve.

She turned and stared at him.

"Didn't you hear me calling?"

She sighed and smiled. "I was deep in a walking meditation," she explained. "I'm sorry."

Up close to her now, with the wind blowing and the darkness falling, Charlie could scarcely contain his joy. But he had no idea what a walking meditation was. Maybe something to do with the mushrooms again.

"Do you remember me?" he asked. "I met you by the diner."

"Yes, I do. Maybe we should introduce ourselves. My name is Diane Riggins."

"Charlie Gravis. Did you just move to Hillsbrook?"

"Oh no. I don't live here. I live in Manhattan. I'm just staying for a while at the Raft, down the road."

"Raft?"

"It's a Buddhist meditation center. I'm on retreat."

All this meant nothing to Charlie. All kinds of strange places had sprung up in Hillsbrook over the past few years.

Trent Tucker started honking his horn.

"Can we give you a lift there—to that raft place?" Charlie offered.

"No, thank you."

"Look," he said, searching for just the right words, "Hillsbrook's a very nice town. Very nice. Can I show you around? Can I buy you dinner? Can I take you—" He clammed up suddenly, knowing he was talking too much and too fast.

She put a hand on his arm. "Listen to me, Mr. Gravis. I think I know what you're saying. I think I know what is in your heart. You want to take me out. You want to talk to me. You want perhaps to hold me—to be with me as a man is with a woman."

She paused there, her hand still on his arm. It was as if he had touched a live wire—electric. He could not quite form the response to what she was saying, but the answer was yes! . . . *yes yes yes!* He wanted all those things. Desperately.

"You seem to be a dear man, Charlie Gravis. But you must understand. I have been through two marriages and many affairs. All that is changed now for me. My next lover, if there will be one, will be a Bodhisattva."

And with this, she kissed him near the chin and walked away.

"Wait!" cried out a bewildered Charlie. He needed to know what kind of a fellow a Bodhisattva was. He had to become one. But his cries were to no avail. She never looked back.

When he climbed back into the truck, a disgusted Trent Tucker said, "An old man like you keeps running out on the road like that and you'll end up like a woodchuck. Squashed. Who was that, anyway?"

Charlie didn't answer. As they neared home, however, he asked the young man: "I don't suppose you know what a Bodhisattva is?"

"Sounds like some kind of baked fish, old man," said Trent Tucker.

* * *

A thin, nervous woman answered the door. Yes, she was Lawrence Eisle's mother. Yes, her son was at home.

It was a dingy floor-through apartment over a convenience store next to a gas station on a county road eight miles northeast of Hillsbrook.

She folded her hands prayerfully as Allie held up his police identification card. "He has done nothing wrong," she said fervently. Then she led him into the living room.

Eisle was stretched out on the sofa. Now Allie remembered the face, but the body had changed. Obviously Eisle had lifted weights in Otisville.

He was wearing a pair of jeans and a Dallas Cowboys hooded sweatshirt. His head was shaved. He was pale and not clean shaven. He wore a tiny silver earring in his left ear.

Eisle's mother showed Allie to a straight-back chair just to the left of the sofa. But she remained standing near the entrance to the room while the two men surveyed each other.

"My name is—" Allie began, but Eisle cut him off.

"I know who you are—and why you're here."

"Ain't you smart," Allie retorted, disliking the young man instantly.

"You wanna know where I was when that cop was shot. The one who busted me."

"And where were you?"

"Right here. Watching TV . . . with my mother."

Allie looked quickly at the woman. She said

nothing, merely looked straight ahead and nodded in affirmation.

The kid stretched, grinning. He's a wise kid, Allie thought. Too wise for his own good.

"To tell you the truth, Sarge—"

"Don't call me Sarge."

"Sure. Anyway, that cop—Chung or Chang or whatever his name was—didn't hassle me too bad. Not compared to the creeps who run the joint at Otisville. But I guess he had to be riding someone's ass pretty bad to get blown away like that. Bam! Now, ain't that right?"

Allie began to perspire. The back of his neck had tightened up.

"Have you been in the town of Hillsbrook lately?" he asked.

"About ten days ago, to buy some magazines."

"That's the only time since you were paroled?"

"Yeah."

"Did you see Officer Chung when you were in Hillsbrook?"

"No."

"Do you own any firearms?"

"No."

"Are there any firearms on the premises?"

"No."

"Ever contact Officer Chung while you were incarcerated?"

"What do I want to do that for?"

"Answer the question."

Eisle began to chuckle, ignoring Allie's order. "And *how* would I do that—even if I wanted to?"

"I told you to answer the question."

"No, of course not."

Lawrence Eisle stretched again, and this time he cracked his knuckles.

"This boring you?" Allie asked, sarcasm and menace at the edge of his voice.

"Wait a minute," Eisle said. "Don't go getting upset. I don't want to give you anything but the truth, the whole truth, and nothing but the truth. I mean, an important dude like yourself gets a little bent out of shape and he starts talking bad shit to my parole officer. Who knows where that's gonna end up? I want us to be tight, you and me. Man, you could be my uncle. You know what I mean?"

"Can I get you a cup of coffee?" Eisle's mother asked Allie.

"No, thanks," Allie said, not looking at her.

"To tell you the truth, Sarge," Eisle continued, "I did send him a valentine once while I was inside. It cost me a carton of smokes to smuggle out."

"A valentine?"

"Yeah. It was a dead rat with some lilies of the valley in its stinking, rotten mouth. Hell, I thought he would dig it. You know how Chinks get off on flowers."

In a fury, moving incredibly fast for the big man that he was, Allie was out of his chair, clutching Eisle's neck with his left hand.

The force of his movement sent the sofa backward. Allie tumbled over. His fingers stayed on the young man's throat.

Only the mother's screams and her fingernails digging into his back brought Allie back to his senses. He staggered away and stared at mother and son as if he had just awakened and found them in his own bedroom.

Then he rushed out of the apartment, out of the building, and into his department-issued car. He drove ten miles at a highly unsafe speed and finally pulled off the road where he collapsed over the wheel.

He awoke from his stupor with the realization that there was another visit he had to make: Sherman Porter.

He was also savvy enough to realize he had severely compromised himself and the investigation by his lunatic behavior back at the Eisle home. He had become for that instant the most pathetic and dangerous creature—a police officer out of control.

Hell, Wynton would have laughed in Eisle's face when he heard the word Chink. But then, Wynton Chung had been young and cool. And if there was one thing Allie Voegler was not, it was cool. He never had been. A bitter laugh broke from his throat. What did Chung's coolness matter now? It didn't help him back there in the parking lot. It had been no defense against that bullet.

He knew he had to get hold of himself. Things were slipping away. He lit a cigarette.

His professionalism had slipped away. Chung had slipped away. And Didi had slipped away. The notion that he would not see her tonight or the next night or any other night was unbearable. And yet it was real. How was he going to get through it? How?

He flung the cigarette butt away and headed for the Ridge.

The section of Hillsbrook called the Ridge was the town's tobacco road. The area itself is a series of small, steep hills. The people who live there are for the most part marginal—laborers, farm workers, domestics, unemployed with a smattering of car thieves. Their homes are trailers and shacks often without electricity or running water.

Sherman Porter owned a once-elegant Winnebago motor home, now on cinder blocks sinking slowly into the autumn mud. During his incarceration, Allie knew, the "home" had been nailed shut.

Now it was open again. And to celebrate his return, Porter had draped the front with an American flag. When he had been a prosperous dairy farmer, he had used the exact same flag on his barn for the Fourth of July and Memorial Day.

It was pitch dark when Allie pulled up. A single light was burning from within. The moment he exited the vehicle he heard music . . . opera . . . *Tosca*, he thought.

He knocked on the door. There was no response. He turned the knob. It was open. There was a stench inside and the place was in total disarray.

"Mr. Porter!" he called out.

A voice from the back answered back loudly: "You bring the check?"

Allie made his way into the cramped sleeping area. Sherman Porter was naked and drunk on a shelf bed, his spindly old legs dangling over the edge of the mattress. The floor was littered with small peach brandy bottles.

"You from Social Security?" Porter yelled over the music. Allie shut off the cassette player before answering.

"No," he said, "I'm from the Hillsbrook Police."

The space was frigid, but the stench remained. All the shutter-type windows were open. Allie closed the two closest to the old man.

"You're going to get pneumonia sitting around like that," he cautioned.

Sherman Porter raised one finger in the air like an academic making a point. "Let me tell you about pneumonia. Hell, I know pneumonia. No different from mastitis in milk cows." He looked for another bottle of peach brandy. He couldn't find one. He waved both arms in futility.

"I haven't been doing too good since I came back from London. Been over in London the last two years. You know that? Pudding and port and Stilton cheese."

"No, Mr. Porter. You've been in a minimum-security facility near Jamestown, New York, for the past two years. You've been locked up."

"You people from Social Security always tell these lies. I mean, why can't you people just act decent?"

"I told you, I'm a Hillsbrook police officer. I'm investigating the murder of Officer Wynton Chung."

"I hate Chinese music," Porter stated. "When I was in London I saw the Peking Opera. Hated it. Like a tractor with bad gears."

Allie started to bring the conversation back to Wynton Chung. Porter flung an empty bottle at him. It missed by a wide margin.

"Leave the check on top of the refrigerator! Put that damn music back on! And get the hell out of here! Or, believe me, I'll call the police."

It was no use, Allie realized. He flipped the music back on and walked out. He felt weary and sad. The debacle with Lawrence Eisle had been bad. But this was worse.

"It's nice. I mean, it's been a long time since you came over in the evening. Not since you and Allie got serious."

Rose Vigdor was talking a mile a minute as she brushed her three dogs. A grim-faced Didi stood close to the barn door listening to the rhythm of the voice while she twirled her Jeep keys. From time to time she stared up at the interior scaffolding of the barn. Like a medieval cathedral, it would never be finished.

Rose's voice dropped an octave. "Is it really over?" she asked Didi.

"Yes. Over. Terminated. Dissolved," Didi answered curtly.

Bozo, the goofy young German shepherd, gave a little growl and snap as the wire brush went over his back.

"Oh, shut up!" Rose said, laughing. "So, Dr. Nightshade, do you like my brushing technique? Notice how I brush all three of them at one time . . . going from one to another."

"What is the point?"

"The point is, my dear scientific friend, that when you brush them one at a time, you diminish the pack solidarity of the dogs. This way, they share the ups and downs together. They moan and whine and snap and beg for more. Pack solidarity, Doctor. The wolf heritage."

"Spoken like a true disciple of Thoreau," Didi replied. "Or maybe Jack London."

Rose paused in the brushing effort to clean the instrument. Then she said, "But you're not here, Didi, to talk about the end of your affair or my brushing technique."

"No, I'm not."

"No. You're here to find out why I never told you about Wynton Chung and me."

"That's right."

"Are you angry?"

"A bit, maybe. But more confused than angry."

"It really wasn't . . . wasn't anything, Didi. Maybe that's why I didn't tell you. It erupted suddenly and flamed out just as quick. It was a fling, that's all. For both of us. I went to his motel five or six times over the past three months. We made love. We laughed. And then it was over. Mainly, I suppose, because I realized he was seeing another woman at the same time."

"Who?"

"I don't know. An older woman."

"Well, Rose, you were older too—older than he was, anyway."

"True. Anyway, it ended a couple of weeks ago. I was going to tell you but I just never got around to it. It was in no way serious. A romp in the hay, as you country gals might say. In fact, I forgot all about him the day after I visited him for the last time. And when he was murdered it was just another cosmic tragedy. I mean, it was just another human being who was destroyed—not my lover. Do you understand?"

"And the chips?"

"I used to bring him bags of my chips when I went to the motel. Just to tease him. Wynton didn't like health foods, so-called. He said they were faddist and dumb."

Huck, the corgi, started moaning. He wanted to be brushed again.

"Go ahead, brush him," Didi urged. Rose obliged. Didi stepped back and watched. Her stomach was doing flips. She knew she wasn't in good shape. This thing with Allie . . . the way it ended . . . the horror of that dance with Chung . . . all of it was beginning to get to her. She really didn't care about Rose's flings. If she told her, fine. If not, fine. She needed Rose. She needed a friend more than ever, and Rose was the only real friend she had.

"Actually," Didi said, "I drove here to get a cup of your miracle tea."

"Aha! The truth is out." Rose put the brush down and laughed. "Which one, Didi? The one that cures depression or the one for cramps?"

"Either/or."

They had their tea together, in front of the wood-burning stove. Outside, a wind began to howl and a mist rolled in, seeping beneath the barn doors and into the barn itself.

For a long time they sat in silence.

"What now, Didi?" Rose finally asked.

"What do you mean?"

"I mean as regards those peculiar bipeds—men."

"Maybe I'll just look for romps in the hay, like someone I know." She meant it humorously but when she saw the shadow cross her friend's face she cursed her big mouth. Obviously the death of Wynton Chung had bitten deeper than Rose admitted.

It was odd, Didi thought, how one of them had slept with Chung on several occasions and the other merely danced with him—once. But it was the latter act that had doomed the young police officer.

Didi finished her tea and said good-bye. The dogs followed her out to the Jeep. She shooed them away and headed back home, driving slowly because of the growing fog. She felt better; the rift with her friend had been healed. She started, almost automatically, to slide one of her Patsy Cline tapes into the deck, then realized she didn't want to hear any sad country music and dropped the tape on the dashboard with the others.

Suddenly a shape loomed out of the darkness into her headlights.

Instinctively she swerved and slammed down on the brake pedal.

The Jeep skidded, spun out, and stalled, throwing Didi to one side of her loosely fastened seat belt.

She sat there, still trying to compose herself. It had all happened so fast. Her shoulder ached a bit. No contact, she thought, a lucky thing. The Jeep had swerved in time. But she had to make sure. She unbuckled the seat belt. Deer on the road in autumn and spring were a well-known hazard around Hillsbrook.

The problem was, it was no deer that had suddenly loomed up. No antlers.

Didi took the flashlight from the glove compartment, switched it on, and gingerly climbed down from the Jeep. She shone the light on the road. No body. No blood. No signs at all. She leaned against the side of the Jeep and switched the flashlight off.

Her relief was matched by her confusion. It had all happened so fast—in a split second. But she could swear that it was a horse and not a deer. She was almost certain she had almost collided with a dappled gray colt. Not a pony; this horse was too big; maybe sixteen hands. And not an Arabian—it was too thick across the chest. Not a Morgan, either—too fine boned. A thoroughbred. Yes. Oh, this was crazy. There were no wild horses in Dutchess County.

She burst out laughing. Maybe, she thought, Rose had spiked that tea.

It was a nightmare. He was being suffocated by a large creature. He didn't know what woke him from that miserable dream. Was it the cramp in his thigh or the jarring phone?

But he jumped up and while reaching for the phone and twisting his body to ease the pain in his cramped thigh, he knocked the clock radio to the floor. It shattered, parts flying every which way.

Joe Gough, Chief of the Hillsbrook Police Department, was on the other end of the line. "Get up! The state troopers have picked up a DWI on the Thruway."

"So?" Allie asked.

"She had a bone-handled snub-nosed .32 in an ankle holster on the floor of the vehicle, Allie."

"Yeah—so?"

"Chung's name was stenciled on the holster strap. Did he have a weapon like that?"

"Yeah."

The cramp had vanished. In its place was a tremor. "But he never carried it," he added.

"Get over there and check it out," the chief barked. "Now!"

Joe Gough hung up. Allie stared at the broken clock radio on the floor. He realized that only the plastic case was out of commission. The digital clock was still operating. It gleamed in the dark room: 4:35 A.M.

Allie dressed, a growing excitement quickening his movements. Maybe it would turn out to be nothing. But maybe it would be very much something. He knew the weapon. He thought Chung kept it in his locker. Chung had only carried it a few times, during his first week on the force, to the derision of his fellow officers. Hillsbrook cops don't carry and don't need backup weapons.

It was a thirty-minute drive to the state trooper barracks just off the Taconic Parkway.

He was ushered into the interrogation room by two troopers, Lofton and Pellegrino, the latter in civvies and carrying a clipboard.

Seated at the table was a disheveled blond woman, about twenty-five. She was wearing a black running suit with gold piping. On her ears were fake gold earrings in the shape of wolf's heads. Biker girl, Allie thought.

She was smoking furiously and she was obviously just coming off some intense boozing. Her name was Della Hope, Allie was informed.

On the table in front of her was a pack of cigarettes, Kools, and the tagged weapon; next to it the unclasped ankle holster.

Even from where he was standing he could see it was Chung's weapon. No doubt about it. He suddenly felt very light-headed and happy. He didn't know why.

Pellegrino motioned for Allie to sit at one of the chairs across from her. He took the other seat. Lofton stood behind Della Hope.

She's weary; she's been around, Allie said to himself. He liked her. He loved Didi but he had always been attracted to a wilder type.

Pellegrino did not introduce Allie to her. He placed the clipboard on the table and consulted it silently.

Della Hope said: "I'm nauseous. I'm going to throw up. And my head hurts."

No one replied.

"What the hell do you people care about my stomach?" she asked. And then laughed at her own question.

Pellegrino took his pencil and tapped the tagged .32. "Tell us about this gun again."

"I told you."

"Tell us again. We forgot."

"He gave it to me."

"Who?"

"Wynton Chung."

"Did you know he was a police officer?"

"Not at the time."

"What time are you talking about?"

"A couple of months ago."

"Where did he give it to you?"

"In Oscar's."

"What is Oscar's?"

"A bar in Kingston."

"You hang out there?"

"Yeah. Sometimes."

"Chung hang out there too?"

"No."

"But he gave you the weapon in there?"

"Right. He was there that night."

"And you knew him?"

"Sure. We were kids together. We used to screw around."

Allie tensed. He had been startled to find out that Rose Vigdor was having an affair with Chung. And this revelation startled him even more. Wynton Chung had always passed himself off as a man with great discipline in regard to women . . . as a young man who selected partners only if they conformed to his laid-back criteria. Neither Rose nor this Della fit.

"Why?" said Pellegrino.

"Why what?" Della Hope said.

"Why did he give you the weapon?"

"He was a little drunk. I told him I was being hassled by an old boyfriend. He gave it to me and told me to blow the sucker away."

Allie bristled. He leaned over and whispered to Pellegrino, "No way. She's lying."

Pellegrino shifted his body away from her and toward him. "You sure?"

Allie spat the words into the trooper's ear: "No way Chung ever told her something like that. No way did he ever speak those words. And he *never* got drunk."

Pellegrino turned back to Della Hope, who was now blowing smoke up at the ceiling.

"Miss Hope, this is Detective Albert Voegler of the Hillsbrook police. He worked with Wynton Chung. He says you're a liar."

"What the hell does he know?" she shot back.

"He knew Wynton Chung well. He worked with him for two years," Pellegrino answered in a calm, rational mode.

The young woman burst into derisive laughter then—bawdy, cruel laughter. When that was finished she closed her eyes and moved her head rhythmically from side to side, listening to some phantom music that no one else could hear. Finally she opened her eyes and stared hatefully at Allie.

"I'll let you in on a little secret about your precious Wynton Chung," she said. "He was nothing but a sleazy creep—just like you."

Allie exploded. Without even thinking, he was on his feet, slamming his open hand into the side of the girl's face. The blow sent her sprawling, blood trickling from her nose. That did not stop Allie; he came right at her again. What would he have done to her if Pellegrino and Loften had not tackled him and wrestled him to the floor as if he were a crazed steer?

He could hear Pellegrino muttering to him over and over, "you idiot, you idiot," as he fought to get free of their weight.

Chapter 4

7:19 A.M.

"Where we headed, Doc?" Charlie Gravis asked as he hoisted his stiff limbs into the red Jeep. By the time he pulled her veterinary bag in after him, she was already turning the motor over.

"To Robert Lorenz's place," Didi answered. "You know him?"

"Met him a few times."

They drove off.

"He's just north of the Juniper Road Fork," she said, situating Lorenz's dairy cow operation geographically for her assistant.

"I'll get you there," Charlie assured her.

They rode in silence for a while. Didi picked up a Patsy Cline cassette and started to insert it into the tape deck. Seeing Charlie wince, she thought better of it.

"Charlie, do you know who his regular vet is? This is the first time he's ever called me."

"I hear he uses the Bracken sisters."

"Oh no!"

"What's the matter with 'em?" he shot back.

"Forget it, Charlie. Just forget it."

But he was still bristling. The Bracken sisters were midwives, herbalists, and even fortune-tellers. They treated people, animals, and anything else they could find—extraterrestrials, for all Charlie knew.

He defended Dr. Nightingale against all comers, but deep in his heart he wouldn't give a plug nickel for scientific veterinarianism. He was an old dairy farmer. Cows ate pasture. Grass fattened them, killed them, cured them. If it didn't grow in the earth, it couldn't be worth much. Not all the antibiotics in the doc's pharmacy were worth one good herbal poultice.

"The fork's coming up. We'll be there in ten minutes," Didi told him.

"Slow down!" Charlie cautioned. "It's a kind of hidden turnoff. Easy to miss."

She slowed the vehicle. With her eyes still fastened on the road ahead, she said in a kindly voice, "Something's been bothering you lately, Charlie. I can see that. Everyone can. I mean, you haven't gone into the kind of tailspin I did after Chung—after the murder—but you're close."

There was no response from him.

"You know"—she pressed on—"if there's anything you need, all you have to do is ask."

"Nothing's bothering me. Just been thinking, that's all."

"Oh . . . okay."

"And thinking makes me tired and kinda sad."

"Okay."

"Let me ask you a question, young doc."

"Sure, Charlie."

"Do you know what a Bodhisattva is?"

Didi looked over at him and then quickly away. "What a strange question for you to—I mean, yes. Sure, I know what it is. At least, I think I do. I took a course in Eastern religions in college. A Bodhisattva is a Buddhist saint. One who postpones his own salvation in order to help others obtain theirs."

Her answer put him in mind of an old hymn. "You mean he don't get his ticket to heaven punched till someone else goes along with him?"

"There isn't any heaven in Buddhism, Charlie. It's more of a non-heaven. A kind of nothing at all."

"Well, that don't make much sense."

"Charlie, I don't have the time to give you a course in Mahayana Buddhism. And I don't remember much of what I learned anyway."

She turned onto the Lorenz property. A big man in a woolen sweater was waiting for them by the fence.

"That's him," Charlie said.

Robert Lorenz shook hands with both the doctor and Charlie. "Leave your Jeep here," he instructed Didi.

They followed him down the path toward the

dairy barn. It was a large edifice. But just as they were upon it, Lorenz changed direction.

"Isn't the cow in the barn?" Didi asked.

Lorenz stopped. "I didn't get you out here to look at a cow."

"But that's what your message said."

"I got a sick baby horse here. A filly. Couple of months old. Something's wrong with her eye. Stomps everyone who comes near her—even her momma."

"Okay," Didi said with a sigh. After all, what did it matter? She was here already.

They headed deeper into Lorenz's property, through a fallow field of alfalfa, into a stand of beech, and finally came to a small paddock area and a shed with stalls.

A bay mare was in the paddock. Didi silently admired her lines. Thoroughbred all the way. And young for a brood mare.

The trio entered the shed area. The foal was in her own stall. A lovely filly—lighter in color than the mother.

"You go near her and she bites, kicks, and butts you with her head. I'm getting worried . . . real worried. That eye's bad," Lorenz said.

Didi nodded. She understood the situation. She'd be worried too if she were in his shoes. Eighty percent of ophthalmic tumors in young horses are malignant. And treatment rarely works, no matter how sophisticated.

She peered through the stall timber rails at the filly who was now kicking out at her feed pail.

Robert Lorenz chewed at his bottom lip for a minute. "I thought," he said, "maybe I could rope her and then you jab a tranquilizer in her rump."

"Let me try something else first," Didi said.

Suddenly her hand caught a splinter on the timber rail. She cursed and pulled away. But then she realized that there were jagged edges all along the wood.

"That filly has been cribbing," she noted.

"Didn't know that," Lorenz replied.

"Here. Take a look. You've got wood chewed away all along the stall."

"Okay," said Lorenz. "I'll get something to put on the wood—vinegar maybe. But let's deal with first things first."

Didi turned away from Robert Lorenz and looked over at her assistant. "Charlie, get me some sugar."

He produced a handful of the oversized white cubes.

Didi palmed three of them and began to undo the stall door.

"Wait a minute!" Lorenz's voice rose in alarm. "What are you doing? I told you that filly is really acting up. She may be a baby but she's big enough to cause you some real damage."

"Take it easy, Mr. Lorenz. I have a way with horses."

And that was the truth; she did. She had always

had a way with fractious equines. She had her own style . . . a method. It was simple, logical, and rarely failed. Don't look at the horse. Don't talk to the horse. Don't approach the horse. Stand still with a few sugar cubes clearly visible in one hand and talk quietly to yourself. It didn't matter what you talked about. Any kind of nonsense would do. Or a poem. Or a nursery rhyme. Even a shopping list. Keep it in a whisper, but keep it audible.

She slid into the stall, walked about a foot deeper, and called out to Charlie: "Have a sponge ready."

Then she went into her act. The filly whinnied and charged her. At the last moment before contact, however, she wheeled away. She did not kick. She had spotted the sugar.

Didi had not budged during the charge. She remained rooted to the spot, telling herself a story about a hen that refused to lay any more eggs because the last three were gold.

The filly charged again, butting Didi in the shoulder with her head. Didi stood fast.

The filly went for the sugar. Didi snapped her fingers. Charlie slipped the large sponge—drenched with an antiseptic painkiller—into the stall.

With the sweep of her arm, Didi sponged the filly's inflamed left eye.

The horse pranced back angrily, chewing one of the sugar cubes. She glared at Dr. Nightingale. Then she seemed to be reflecting on the change for the better in her eye. Then, apparently quite happy about the whole thing, she ambled over in search of another sugar cube.

But it was all gone. Didi, now outside the stall, showed the sponge to Lorenz. It was dotted with tiny specks.

"She's been cribbing too much. On young wood. All kinds of sawdust and chips were flying up into her eyes while she was biting and chewing. It accumulates, you know."

She went back into the stall with more sugar and a fresh sponge. There was no problem at all now. The filly was downright affectionate.

"Turn her back out with her mother," Didi said as she exited the stall after having thoroughly cleaned both the filly's eyes.

"Will do," the dairy farmer said, and began to thank her profusely.

"Mr. Lorenz," Didi said, cutting him off, "why build stalls all the way out here? Why not near the cow barn where you work most of the time?"

"That's just the way it turned out," he explained. "But you're right. It doesn't make a whole lot of sense."

Later, as they headed home, Didi remarked to Charlie, "Young horses usually don't crib."

"She must've been chewing that wood like it was corn on the cob," he noted.

"You know, no one has ever identified the cause of cribbing. Some people think it's simply a form of equine neurosis. Some say it's a dysfunctional

endocrine system. And some claim it's just an in-
born response to nausea—just as dogs go to grass
when they're nauseous, horses chew wood. Take
your pick."

"I think it's just that they're stupid."

"Maybe," she mused. "By the way, I wanted to
ask you something. Did you ever hear talk of wild
horses in the Hillsbrook area? Roaming around
free, I mean. Literally wild."

"No. Never heard of one. Never saw one. I do remember hearing about something when I just got
back from the war. A couple of plow horses
slipped their traces and ran off. They ended up in
the church cemetery, eating up a storm. I guess the
pasture over graves is sweet."

"I'm talking about a young, wild, dappled gray
colt, Charlie."

"Ha! This ain't Wyoming, young doc."

Allie walked out of the state trooper barracks.
His right ear was caked with dried blood and the
side of his face bruised from contact with the table
after he had been wrestled to the floor.

He saw the Hillsbrook police cruiser and walked
very slowly over to it.

Chief Gough was on the passenger side. Officer
Brasco was behind the wheel.

The moment he reached Gough's rolled-down
window, the chief began to yell. "What the hell is
the matter with you?"

"I'm sorry. I just lost it in there. I don't know what happened. I've been feeling weird lately."

Gough got out of the car and slammed the door behind him.

He moved closer to Allie, pugnacious, furious, his fists balled as if he were going to strike the detective.

"The troopers are not going to let this one slide," he said.

"I didn't think they would," Allie admitted. "But I didn't mean to hit her, Chief. Believe me, I just—"

"Shut up and listen!" Gough barked, poking the much taller Allie in the breastbone with two fingers. "I'm going to lay out a number of procedures for you to follow. If you follow them to the letter, there is a chance—a slim chance—that you'll still be a police officer when this is over. Are you hearing me?"

Allie nodded.

"First. You go back to Hillsbrook and put your weapon in your locker. As of this moment you are on administrative suspension, with full pay. Understand?"

"Yes."

"Second. Get out of the Hillsbrook area until this blows over. I don't want you speaking to anyone. Do you have a place to stay?"

"I guess so. There's an old marine buddy of mine in Cooperstown. He'll put me up probably."

"Good. Go there direct from headquarters."

Chief Gough pulled a small folded piece of paper out of his shirt pocket and handed it to Allie.

"Next . . . you make an appointment to see this lady whose name and phone number are on this paper. She's a headshrinker for the state troopers. When a cop goes around the bend she's the one they see. And let's face facts, Voegler, if you ain't around the bend now, you soon will be. Besides, you're going to need her if this goes to a full hearing. Got all that?"

"Yes."

"Check in every day with headquarters. And I mean every day. Got that?"

"Yeah, I got it."

"In addition, if from this second forth you are seen in a bar or purchasing or imbibing any alcoholic beverage whatever—you are through. Understood?"

"I wasn't drinking, Chief. I got here at five in the morning. You spoke to me on the phone. You woke me. Sure, I had a few beers last night but . . ."

Allie's words trailed away when he saw that Gough was not listening to him. He was scuffing his shoes on the gravel parking lot and squinting past him, into the sun.

"Okay," Allie said quietly. "I won't miss a beat."

Gough turned, strode to the car, and got in. It roared off.

Allie headed slowly for his own vehicle. Just as he opened the door he saw the Hillsbrook police cruiser U-turn, double back, and head toward him.

Brasco braked only five feet away from him amid a swirl of gravel.

Gough rolled down the window and said in a loud voice tinged with a kind of official sarcasm: "You *do* understand that in addition to everything else, vis-à-vis the department and the troopers you are looking at assault charges. You do realize that, don't you, Voegler?"

"I do."

"That's swell. One other thing: Chung's father wants his son's effects. What did you find in his motel room? You conducted a search of the premises, didn't you?"

"Yes. There were some clothes. But no private stuff. No papers, photos, bills."

"Any idea where he kept it?"

"No."

The car drove off again. Allie saw a face staring at him from inside the barracks. It looked like Trooper Pellegrino, but he couldn't be sure. He lit a Newport and smoked it, leaning against his vehicle, his back to the face. Detective Albert Voegler felt like he was three steps from the grave. He wondered what Didi's reaction would be when she heard what he had done. He wondered whether she would realize it was the first time he had ever struck a woman. He wondered whether it mattered. As for Gough, well, he was tough but better than Leavis, his predecessor, who was a fool.

* * *

Ike Badian removed his cigar, spat, and said to Charlie Gravis: "My prediction is that it's going to turn cold real soon."

Charlie, leaning on the fence, smoking one of Ike's cigars, listened and didn't comment. Ike's small herd was in the pasture, in front of them.

Having made the prediction, Ike changed the subject. "What do you make of that Voegler fellow? Your boss' boyfriend. I heard on the radio he's been suspended. He beat up a girl witness in the state trooper barracks. The guy must be nuts."

"He has been nuts since that friend of his was shot. But the doc and him called it quits a few days ago," Charlie explained.

"You like the cigar?"

"Not bad."

"I'm buying them now by mail, from Connecticut. Ten boxes at a time."

"Good for you."

"Look at Sophie! Look at her!" Ike shouted suddenly, pointing to one of his cows who had sat down majestically in the field.

"I'm looking. So what?"

"I don't know. I just like to watch her sit down. She thinks she's a goddamn queen. Maybe it's because she knows her milk is now going to the new yogurt factory near Binghamton."

Charlie lowered his tone. "Ike, I want to talk to you about something serious."

"Uh-oh. When I hear that tone of voice I get worried. I say to myself 'Watch out, Ike! Charlie Gravis is heading into one of his crazy schemes and he wants to drag you along.' But get this, Charlie: whatever you're up to this time—I want no part of it. Even if you promise me ten thousand dollars a month and Fidel Castro's humidor."

"Does he have a humidor?"

"Who the hell knows?"

"It's no scheme, Ike. I met a woman near the diner. I fell in love. I can't think straight. I can't put the right shoe on the right foot. I feel sometimes like I'm flying and sometimes like I'm sinking. The real bad part, Ike, is that she wants no part of me."

"Bad break, Charlie. But if a guy your age falls that hard, it may be early Alzheimer's."

"She's a Buddhist."

"Oh . . . that ain't so bad."

"She's about fifty."

"Too young for you, Charlie."

"She's just in Hillsbrook for a retreat. She lives in Manhattan."

"Forget her."

"But she likes me. She says she likes me. But she won't go out with me. Listen to this, Ike. She's saving her love for a Bodhisattva."

"You lost me on that one."

"A Buddhist saint."

"Sounds like an old Mills Brothers song. 'I'm Saving My Love for a Body . . . A Bodysanna' . . . or whatever. Remember the Mills Brothers, Charlie?"

"I do not know one damn thing about Buddhism," Charlie cried out.

Ike Badian was startled by the emotion in his friend's declaration of ignorance.

"Calm down," he said.

"She isn't beautiful, Ike. That's not it. But there is something about the way she looks and talks, and the way she touched me . . . it just takes my breath away."

"Like emphysema," Ike noted, smirking.

"I haven't thought about sex like I've been thinking about it lately since I was forty years old."

"Only the lonely," said Ike.

"I've been thinking. Maybe I should find out something about this Buddhism."

"If the lady doesn't want you, she can make up all kinds of excuses. Like when Sophie won't let her milk down."

Charlie stared grimly out onto the pasture.

"You remember my sister, Charlie? May she rest in peace."

"You mean the crazy one?"

"That's right. Lottie."

"Been dead a long time."

"Not that long. Twelve years this December fourth. Anyway, if I remember, when she died she was a Christian Scientist. But before that, she was a Jehovah's Witness, a Roman Catholic, a Hindu, a foot-washing Baptist, and even a Mormon. I'm pretty sure she was a Buddhist once too. I mean she used to go through religions like I go through cigars."

"So what?"

"Well, when she converted from one religion to another, she always bought books to read on the new one. And they're all in my attic. In cardboard boxes. You want to take some of the Buddhist ones, help yourself."

"Thanks, Ike. Maybe I will."

The man on the other end of the phone was unfriendly, suspicious. His name was Art Moldava and when Didi had heard the news of the assault on the radio and couldn't reach Allie at his apartment or at police headquarters, she figured he had gone to Cooperstown. Moldava was the only friend Allie had. Where else could he go?

"I'm not a reporter. I'm not a lawyer. I'm not a cop," Didi said.

"Who the hell are you then?"

"His ex-fiancée."

"Ain't that sweet?" Moldava said. "Send Allie some flowers. I'll make sure he puts them in water."

"Is he okay?"

There was no answer on the other end of the phone.

"You're a fool!" Didi suddenly shouted into the receiver. Then she realized this was the wrong tack to take.

"Listen, please . . . just give Allie a message.

From Nightingale to Voegler. It's three-twenty now. Tell him I'll be waiting for him in that donut shop on Route 28 about five miles west of Kingston. It's on the north side of the highway. He knows it. I'll be there about two hours from now. I want to see him. I want to talk to him. Will you tell him that?"

"Anything you say, lady," was the laconic response. The phone line went dead. Would he deliver the message? Didi had to act based on the premise that he would, and that Allie would show. She had no choice.

She drove slowly to the meeting place. It was a bitter, lonely trip. Her guilt was overpowering. She had known Allie was distraught after the Chung murder. Why hadn't she been able to deal with it? Why had she let his erratic behavior and accusations trigger a breakup? He needed help—not schoolgirl revenge. She wasn't a little girl anymore. She was a grown woman with a practice, a household of retainers, and a keen sense of responsibility. She had treated hundreds of distraught cows, horses, dogs, goats, and God knew what else. Many of them had been violent as a result of the pain from their infirmities. But she had never held them responsible for acts committed in that state.

Why hadn't she been able to extend that simple courtesy to her lover?

It was the breakup at Rose's place, she knew, that had sent him over the edge in that state trooper barracks. Allie Voegler was a big rough man who hunted deer in season and sometimes drank to excess. He had many faults, but brutality was not one of them. Nor was stupidity.

She grew more nervous as she approached the meeting place. Maybe it had closed down, she thought. Maybe Allie wasn't at his friend's place at all. Maybe. Maybe. Maybe.

In fact, the donut place was still there, freshly painted. And it had expanded, swallowing the hardware store. There were tables in the center and ledges and stools along the windows.

He was seated at the last stool, wearing a checked flannel jacket and staring down into a cup of coffee on the ledge.

The sight of him made her legs weak. She had never seen him looking so lost, so terrible—his face pale, shoulders hunched like a wounded bear's.

Recovering, she walked quickly to him and sat on the next stool. She took his hand and pressed it against her cheek.

"I'm going to be okay," he said simply.

"Sure, you are."

"Just a thorn in the paw."

She smiled and let his hand fall. He put his arm around her.

"I'm too ashamed to apologize, Dr. Nightingale."

"Nobody apologizes to vets," she replied. Then she added, "What's done is done, Allie. No apologies. No explanations. No public confessions. No nothing. Just tell me what I can do to help."

"I'll be staying with Art."

"Yes. I figured that out."

"There'll be a hearing. Maybe a grand jury."

"Tell me what you want me to do."

"You've done it. You're here."

She went and got two fresh coffees and two glazed whole wheat donuts. He didn't drink his coffee or taste the donut. Nor did she. They sat in silence, shoulder to shoulder, touching.

"I have to go to a shrink," he finally said.

"There are worse things."

He leaned over and kissed her on the neck. It was sexual.

"Not here, Allie," she said softly.

He sat back, chastised. Then, drawing a deep breath, he told her: "I'm lying, Didi. And I don't like lying to you."

"Lying about what?"

"There is something I need. Now."

"What?"

"Information."

"Keep talking, Allie."

"I want you to go to the Whitetail Inn."

"Where Wynton was living?"

"Yeah. His personal belongings were not in the room. Nothing but some clothes, toiletries, and bags of those stupid chips. There's a clerk at the motel. His name is Gillespie, I think. Talk to him.

Shake him up. Find out what he knows. Where the hell is Wynton's stuff?"

Didi stared down into her coffee. She didn't reply.

"I'm suspended, Didi. Maybe I'll lose my job. Maybe I'll end up in jail. Or a nut ward. But Chung is in the grave. And you, me, and the whole world put him there."

"I understand," she said, "believe me, I understand. But there are seven other able bodies in the Hillsbrook Police Department. It's their job, Allie."

"No! I got a bad feeling about all this. I have a feeling that the bullet that killed him came from outside Hillsbrook . . . that something is out there that no Hillsbrook cop can deal with."

"Even you, Allie?"

"Well, look at me," he replied caustically.

Didi took a bite of the donut. It wasn't bad.

"I'll make that house call," she said.

Chapter 5

Didi wheeled the Jeep into the courtyard of the Whitetail Inn. It was a gloomy fall morning.

She shut the ignition off. Rose Vigdor, in the passenger seat, asked, "Are you sure you want me along on this?"

"I'm sure."

Rose shook her head sadly.

"Was it five times? Or ten times? Isn't that strange, Didi? I can't remember how many visits I made to Wynton Chung's room."

"Let's go."

"Wait a minute."

Didi looked at her friend. "What's the matter?"

"Tell me. Why did he live in this dump?"

"I don't know, Rose. But before this he had a nice small apartment in town, in one of those big old boardinghouses at the end of Main Street. Allie told me it was nice anyway."

They walked inside. A tall, wispy young man with a purple tie and a crooked collar was reading the newspaper behind a counter. On the walls of the small motel office were photos of a bygone era: hunters displaying trophy bucks.

"Are you Mr. Gillespie?" Didi asked.

He straightened up and looked them over. "I am," he said. "You the police?"

Rose laughed. "Do we look like police?"

"I've seen you before."

"That well may be," Rose answered.

He folded the newspaper. "Room?" he inquired, now all business.

"No," Didi said. "We're friends of Wynton Chung. He had some legal papers of ours. He told us he stored all his valuables in the motel office."

"He told you wrong. We don't store anything for guests."

"Why would he tell us that, then?" Didi snapped.

"You'd have to ask him."

"He's dead."

"Yes. That's the point. You're going to have to take my word for it. The police did, and so do you." Then he angrily opened the paper. "I don't like it when people call me a liar," he mumbled.

"I'm not calling you a liar, Mr. Gillespie. Maybe it was some other clerk on a different shift who agreed to store the things for him."

That was the wrong thing to have said.

"I am no *clerk*. I'm the manager. And I put in eighteen-hour shifts six days a week. Right now, when I'm not here the office is shut. Understand?"

Rose pulled at Didi's arm, her way of saying that

it was time to go, that the situation had reached a level of vituperation making further progress impossible. Rose, despite her nature-girl facade, was ever the realist.

Didi started to exit, but she stopped on a dime before she reached the door. Her face was lit up with that strange smile, as if she had suddenly diagnosed a very perplexing bovine disorder.

"What is it?" Rose had nearly tripped over Didi, who was frozen in place.

"There's something else we should ask Mr. Gillespie."

They approached the counter again, not deterred by the manager's stern look.

"One thing more, Mr. Gillespie," Didi said. "Perhaps Wynton Chung entrusted the papers to the woman who used to visit him here."

The manager smiled. It was a smile that said managers who rent rooms by the hour hear nothing, see nothing, and say nothing.

"She was an older woman, much older than Chung," Didi said, remembering what Rose had told her. When she spoke those words to Gillespie, Rose looked very unhappy.

The manager continued reading his newspaper. His smile had become a smirk.

Didi reached into her pocket, pulled out her wallet, and extracted one of her business cards. She had ordered some 2,000 of them when she started her practice and she still had 1,966 left. She put the card down on the newspaper.

"Mr. Gillespie"—she spoke in her best stable-side manner—"my family has been in Hillsbrook a long time. I make my living treating milk cows and horses and pigs. I am not a process server. I am not a lawyer or a private investigator. I am a neighbor of yours who is just trying to—"

She didn't get to finish her speech. Gillespie picked up the card and in a fury ripped it in half. "Spare me the list of your credentials," he said bitterly. "I don't care if you're a member of the Hillsbrook chapter of the DAR. I don't care if you're the Florence Nightingale of all the wounded cows in Dutchess County.

"Now listen carefully, because I'll only say this once. What I told you was the truth. We do not keep valuables or anything else for our guests. We don't let them put so much as a chocolate bar in the office refrigerator. Okay?

"As for the women in Mr. Chung's life . . . well, all right, the man is dead. I'll say that I do remember *one* older woman visiting him."

He paused then and gave Rose a sly look. She stood there stonily.

"I don't know this older lady's name. Visitors don't register with the desk, only clients. She might have been twenty years older than he. Maybe more. All I really recall is that she came to the motel in a blue Volvo that had seen better days; it was a mess. She was a tall woman, extremely thin, and a little stooped. That is all. Are you happy now?"

"Happy enough," Didi said as she turned away.

She did not speak again until she and Rose had settled themselves in the Jeep. She slipped the key into the ignition but did not turn it.

"Can you imagine it?" she finally said to Rose.

"Imagine what?"

"All the time he was sleeping with you, he was carrying on an affair with Ruth Stringfellow."

Alone in his tiny room, the door shut, the sounds from the kitchen only a distant murmur, Charlie Gravis sat down on the cot that served as his bed and examined the book he had taken from Ike Badian's attic.

It was a small, odd shaped paperback with a thick, yellowish cover. There had been so many books to choose from up in the attic, several of them about this thing called Buddhism.

He had selected this particular volume for several reasons, none of which had anything to do with the book's contents.

First of all, the title was intriguing: *Look in the Mirror and See Nothing*. And in smaller type, the subtitle: *The Message of Gotama Buddha*.

Second, the author's name was funny: Lady Vivian Pelt Barraclough.

Third, the book had been published in Sheffield, England, of all places. Sheffield—Charlie remembered that that was where good knives used to be made.

Fourth, the book was published in 1924, the very year he was born.

And finally, it seemed to have been printed and bound in the cellar of someone who was mighty tipsy at the time.

Charlie opened the book, frowning as he skimmed the Introduction. He skipped to the first page of Chapter 1.

"Look in the mirror," he read aloud.

Charlie looked up. In fact there was a mirror on the back of his bedroom door, an elongated, cracked old thing with a mildewed wooden frame—but a mirror nonetheless.

He followed the author's instructions. Looking at his reflection, he saw himself sitting on the bed with the book in his hands. He returned to the text.

No doubt you see a man or a woman with a unique body and soul, who lives in such and such a place at such and such a time. No doubt you see a man or woman who has experienced joys and sorrows, successes and failures, love and hate, truth and lie, spiritualities and sensualities.

He looked into the mirror once more, muttered "Ain't that the truth," and returned to the text.

"Siddhartha Gotama, the Buddha, born in the sixth century B.C. in what is now Nepal, takes issue with you.

"What you see in the mirror, he says, is an illusion. He says, 'The body, monks, is not a self.' He reveals that no self and no lasting soul can be found in you. He reveals that what you just saw in the mirror is simply a bundle of phenomena temporarily joined into a pattern.

"*You* have no essence. *You* have no eternal anything. You differ from a beetle or a sow or a tree only in the temporary pattern of your atoms. You are a random puzzle put together by you-don't-know-who . . . to be dissolved and rearranged by you-don't-know-who—or when."

Charlie put the book aside. He was a bit disturbed by what he had read. These people are crazy, he thought. He wished he had the guts to light a cigar, but he knew the smoke would curl out under the door and bring the wrath of Mrs. Tunney down on his head. He stared glumly at the ugly little book. This kind of stuff set him on edge. Like you felt when you were getting the flu. Then he had a sharp memory of Diane Riggins walking along the road in her yellow slicker. He shook his head ruefully, picked up the book again, and once again began to read.

"Because you are living with these illusions, you do not understand the nature of existence.

"Gotama reveals it. 'This is the noble truth of suffering . . . birth is suffering . . . grief, lamentation, pain, affliction and despair are suffering . . . to be united to what is unloved is suffering . . . to be separated from what is loved is suffering . . . not to obtain what is longed for is suffering.'

"Like Gotama's monks, dear reader, you are no doubt wondering from whence comes all this suffering. It comes from craving. And the extinction of craving will end all suffering and all illusion.

"How does one extinguish craving? By holding to these noble truths—as you walk and as you sit; as you breathe in and breathe out. By treating every other bundle of phenomena—dogs, vultures, worms, human murderers, acorns—with compassion for their suffering existence and loving-kindness.

"When you have applied yourself with diligence, all illusions and sorrow will vanish with the cravings. And you will look in the mirror and see nothing. You will have reached *Nibbana*."

Charlie grunted. Nibbana? It sounded like a breakfast cereal or one of those loud rock bands Trent Tucker listened to. But Charlie kept reading.

"Then you can turn your wisdom into a raft to help others reach the radiant shore of *Nibbana*. You can become a Bodhisattva."

In a sudden rage at seeing the name of his rival in love pop up, Charlie flung the book at the old mirror.

What the hell were these people talking about? he wondered. He lay down unhappily and pulled at a dry cigar.

"Isn't it strange that the Stringfellows, who are supposed to have all kinds of money, have the same car as me, a poor little city girl alone in the wilderness?"

Didi laughed. "No, Rose. That surely is a blue Volvo and it's surely beat-up, but it's still ten years newer than your heap."

"Volvo owners are very fond of their cars," she said dreamily.

The Jeep was parked across the road from the fence that separated the Fox property from that of the Stringfellows. The Volvo was halfway between the road and the Stringfellow house.

"Are we going in there?" Rose asked.

"Yes. But you can wait out here."

"Why are you going in?"

"I could give you a lot of reasons, Rose."

"Such as?"

"For one, Allie asked me to find Chung's personal things. It's plausible that this Ruth Stringfellow has some information on that. For another thing, I find the whole idea of a passionate relationship between this woman and Wynton Chung astonishing. There must be more to it than meets the eye. And finally, to be honest with you, Rose—since you were involved with the man and I danced him to his death and Allie has cracked up over the whole mess—I don't see how any of us can leave any of it alone."

Rose thought it over a minute. "You're right, Nightingale. You're right—again."

They left the car and walked to the front door of the large, somewhat ramshackle house and rang the bell. Once. Twice. Three times. In another minute they heard footsteps approaching, and then Ruth Stringfellow opened the door.

Tall and stooped, yes. Gillespie was right about that. But, up close, she had a kind of fierce beauty, much like a large winged bird. Her garments were strange: a maroon-colored robe with deep pockets and high collar. Like a bathrobe for a czar, Didi thought.

"Yes?"

Didi started to introduce herself, but Mrs. Stringfellow cut her off. "I know who you are. My husband and I made inquiries after you and your assistant looted our shrubbery."

"Looted! Mrs. Stringfellow, those plants were poisonous. They nearly wiped out your neighbor's herd."

"It serves him right," she said saltily. "Let him keep his fencing intact."

"I know he's to blame. You are right. And I know I should have asked your permission before I removed those plants. But I was told this was basically a summer residence, that you and your husband were not around."

"You were misinformed." Ruth Stringfellow turned her attention to Rose then. "And who is this—another assistant? How many do you have?"

Rose shyly identified herself as "just a neighbor from down the road, ma'am." Her phony self-deprecation almost made Didi wince. For a minute she thought Rose might end her act with a humble curtsy. It was another instance of Rose's strange sense of humor emerging in a tense situation.

"Never mind that now," the woman said contemptuously. "What do you want now? Looking to strip more greenery from my property? What are you doing, selling it to landscape gardeners?"

Didi, though she tried hard not to, lost her temper then. "Yes!" she snapped. "I'm making a fortune. But at the moment I'm interested in a little poison ivy. Like your relationship with Wynton Chung."

The tall woman paled. Her grip tightened on the edge of the door. Suddenly there was fear in her eyes. But the she reined in her panic and said in a low, controlled voice, "I know no such person."

"Of course you do," Didi said with a sneer. "The murdered Hillsbrook police officer."

"I've heard of the tragedy, yes," Ruth Stringfellow said coldly, "but I did not know Officer Chung personally."

"Then why did you make those visits to his room at the Whitetail Inn?"

"I don't know what you mean. I've never been to any Whitetail Inn."

"Not true. We have a witness who says you visited him several times."

The woman's jaw tightened. "I never went to any motel and I had no acquaintance with that young man. I have no idea what you're talking about. No idea—do you understand me? Now it's time you left my property."

Ruth Stringfellow was holding herself stiffly, willing her hands to remain at her side. She was in control, but Didi had the sense that she was very close to tears.

"Are you sure you want to stick to that story, Mrs. Stringfellow?" Didi asked.

The woman's face relaxed then, and she smiled sadly as she shut the door softly in their faces.

Rose and Didi walked back to the Jeep where they sat in silence for a long time.

"She's a married woman," Didi said at last. "Naturally she had to lie. But there's also something pathetic about her."

"Yes . . . *if* she's lying," Rose commented.

Didi turned on her in a fury. "Damn you, Rose! Be serious. Of course she's lying. That's the problem with this thing. Everybody seems to be lying about Chung."

Color sprang to Rose's face. "Are you saying that *I* lied to you?"

"Well, you kept your affair with him a secret, didn't you? And then when you were forced into telling me, what you said was so vague as to be worthless."

"Oh come on, Didi. I told you what happened. I used to run into him in Harland Frick's health food store in town. We used to chat. Then he just seemed to want it to go further. Well, so did I; we both did. I went to bed with him a few times and it was nice. But I felt I had to end it when I found out he was having an affair with someone else at the same time. It's a pretty common story.

"So just what are you accusing me of here? What is it you think I'm hiding? Maybe I should have told you about it from the beginning. I didn't. I'm sorry—okay? How many times do you want me to apologize? How many—"

"Wait a minute, wait a minute!" Didi said, holding up her hand to stem the flow of the other one's words. "You're talking too fast."

Rose pouted.

"Rose, you never told me you used to see Wynton in the health food store."

"Didn't I? I thought I did."

"No, you didn't, Rose!" she shouted.

"So sue me, Didi!" Rose stormed back. "I'm telling you now, aren't I?"

Exasperated, Didi began to speak very slowly and deliberately. "Look, Rose, didn't it seem kind of strange to you?"

"What?"

"That Wynton Chung would be hanging out in Harland's store. I mean, you yourself said he had nothing but contempt for health food and those who ate it. He never touched the chips you brought to his motel room."

"Oh."

"Yes. 'Oh.' "

Rose squirmed in her seat. "I guess you have a point. It is strange, now that you bring it up."

"Right. When cows graze in pasture they don't like, you'd better pay attention."

"All right, Doctor, you've made your point."

"Maybe we'd better pay your good friend Harland Frick a visit."

Rose looked troubled, but she agreed. "Maybe we should."

Why don't I take a walk? Charlie Gravis asked himself.

In Didi's clinic office, which was attached to the main house, Charlie was monitoring the phones.

But no calls were coming in. And if they did come, Charlie reasoned, the machine would pick them up. Besides, the boss was gallivanting about somewhere and couldn't be reached.

So he started out on his constitutional. Charlie was a bit embarrassed as he strode onto the road in the early afternoon sun and headed north, toward the town. After all, Hillsbrook people—natives, that is—didn't go strolling on the roads. They got into their vehicles and drove.

And he, above all, hadn't taken a stroll on a Hillsbrook road since he last got drunk, which was a very long time ago.

Not only was he embarrassed, he was a bit grim. He wasn't fooling himself. The only reason he thought of taking a stroll was the possibility that he would see Diane Riggins again. Imagine it: Charlie Gravis wandering the countryside like that damn fool, Bert Conyers, who was mad as a hatter.

He kept his head turned away from the road as he walked so the drivers in the passing cars would not recognize him and stop to offer him a lift. But, in fact, few cars were on the road.

He tried to increase his speed, but he became winded and had to slow his pace. It was odd looking at the terrain from this perspective. Again he had the feeling of having awakened in a place that was not Hillsbrook. Oh, the land itself hadn't changed much. But everything else had. The people and animals that used to live there had vanished. The old barns were empty or had been converted to pottery shops. New homes lay on old slopes. Renovated houses flashed new paint from old groves. It was as if there had been a thorough shuffling of the deck. As though some capricious god above had said, "Well, we'll keep the grass, but everything on the grass has to be changed."

As he passed a place, he ticked off in his head the family who used to live there. He could even recall the size of their dairy herd.

Still, all these thoughts about the past did not sadden him. Dairymen loathed sentiment. You couldn't exist in the illogical world of the milk cow if you were a sentimental fool.

Suddenly, ahead of him, he saw movement . . . a glint . . . a flash of color. His heart leaped about in his chest.

But no—it wasn't a yellow slicker that he had seen.

Hopes deflated, he walked steadier. There seemed to be some kind of nonhuman tumult on the other side of the road. Charlie crossed over to get a closer look.

A red-tailed hawk had pulled a roadkill woodchuck off the tar and into a shallow ditch.

The hawk was trying to eat his prize but was now being harassed by five, six, a dozen crows that darted and nibbled and pecked at the carrion while avoiding the flailing wings and talons of the defending hawk.

Charlie stood still. He watched and listened. It was a raucous primal scene, the hawk becoming more and more furious and charging various crows—only to hurry back as other crows attacked the carrion.

It was strange. He had come upon scenes like this all his life. A thousand times maybe. What person raised in the country had not? Sure, different kinds of hawks, perhaps. Different kinds of roadkill, perhaps. And maybe ravens rather than crows. But it was the same essential struggle.

This time, however, as he watched the unfolding scene, he felt a terrible sorrow. It seemed to grow in him . . . to fatigue him . . . to crawl into his bones so that he could scarcely stand.

It was as though he was seeing this kind of thing for the first time. The woodchuck had died because he craved something on the other side of the road. The hawk had gathered the dead creature off the road because he craved meat. The crows had mounted their assault because they craved carrion.

And he, Charlie, had come upon them because he had gone for a walk in search of love.

Some of the words he had read in the crazy Englishwoman's book came to him: "This, monks, is the noble truth of suffering."

But he couldn't remember any more. He started to cross the road. But he couldn't leave. He felt drawn to those struggling creatures. To those—as Lady Barraclough referred to them—bundles of phenomena.

I, Charlie Gravis, am just a random bundle of short-lived phenomena. No different from the hawk. Or the crow. Or the woodchuck.

Another fierce memory invaded him: Diane talking about the random glory of the mushroom spores. Yes! He understood now what she had been saying!

But he was becoming dizzy. He turned and dropped in sections, like a construction crane. I'll rest here for a minute, he thought, his eyes on the crows. Then he lost consciousness.

"Was I asleep? Or knocked out?" he asked himself twenty minutes later as he opened his eyes in the shallow ditch.

He rose, brushed himself off, and looked about him. The hawk and the crows were gone. There was little left of the woodchuck.

"Brother woodchuck," he heard himself saying, "this is the noble truth of suffering . . ."

As before, he could not remember further.

But he was suddenly suffused with a wave of compassion for brother woodchuck. So powerful was this wave, so overtaking, that he was frightened he would lose consciousness again.

So he turned and began to trot home—like an old man chasing his youth.

Many people in Hillsbrook thought that the little old man with the broken blood vessels on his nose and the tufts of white hair dotting his almost bald skull was quite mad.

But there were some others (not many, but some) who considered Harland Frick, proprietor of the only health food store in town, to be a historian of note.

For it was said that he knew more about Hillsbrook and its people than anyone else, and he knew not just who married whom or who died when; he knew all the secret things.

There was tension between Didi and Rose as the two entered Frick's shop: Rose flat-out revered the old man, but Didi's feelings about him were, at best, ambivalent. But it had been decided outside that it would be Rose who would conduct the questioning, particularly after she had dropped one more nugget of information during the ride from the Stringfellow place into town. Harland Frick, she admitted, knew about her affair with Chung. He was the only one who did know, other than herself. Rose had confided in him.

Harland greeted them robustly. He was always happy to see people—customers or just visitors. He sat behind his desk, going over his bills, and motioned for them to take chairs or park themselves on an unopened crate, of which there were many.

"I told Didi about Wynton and me," Rose said sheepishly.

"Well, good," Harland said, nodding. "Your friend should know."

"I told her how I used to see him here all the time."

"That you did," he said. "That you did. A lot of people did. But, you know, I never met one person anywhere who didn't like Wynton Chung." Harland sharpened a pencil, then he continued, "He was always right on the money—if you know what I mean. And there wasn't a cruel bone in his body. I'm going to miss him."

Rose started to say something, stopped herself, fiddled around with some cans of unsalted organic peanuts, and then finally stammered out what she had wanted to say in the first place: "Harland, Didi thinks it's strange that he hung out in here so often."

"Why can't Didi speak for herself? I'm looking right at Dr. Nightingale."

"All right," said Didi, addressing Harland's

question. "Rose got it right. Wynton hated health foods. He even scorned people who ate yogurt. So what was he doing here? Unless he took an interest in local Hillsbrook history—maybe the eighteenth century?"

"No. I never talked to him about the town's history."

"He wouldn't have stayed in Hillsbrook," Rose added. "He wanted to work in a big city. He wanted to be a real cop in the real world, he always said."

"This is about as real as it gets," Didi remarked curtly to her friend. Then she said to Frick, "Do you understand my confusion?" She realized Rose would be of no help at all in this situation.

"Maybe"—the old man tweaked his young interrogator—"he just liked to talk to me."

"Don't get me wrong, Harland. No doubt he did like you. If one wants gossip, you have it. If one wants genealogies, you have those. If one wants old scandals, you know where the bodies are buried—so to speak. But still, I just have the feeling Chung wasn't hanging around here because of your genius as an oral historian."

Harland Frick looked pained. He studied the pencil he had sharpened. Then he laid it down on the desk, fastidiously. He didn't say a word in response to Didi's comment.

"This is important," she prompted.

He seemed to mull over her claim. Then he asked, "Oh? Why is that?"

"Because he's dead. Because he was murdered. Because now every relationship of any kind he had in Hillsbrook is . . . how shall I put it, Harland, if you don't like the word 'important'? What about 'interesting'?"

Harland answered Didi, but as he did so he looked at Rose.

"Okay," he began. "It was simple. I cashed checks for him."

"You mean his personal checks?" Didi asked.

"No."

"What, then? Payroll?"

"No, not that either."

"Then what? *What*, Harlan?"

"Checks from—other people. Made out to him. He'd endorse them and give them to me. I would double endorse them and deposit them in my account, giving him the cash. Commercial accounts still accept double endorsed checks around here."

"But why didn't he just deposit them in his own account? Why not go to the bank?"

"He said it was because people might misunderstand."

"Misunderstand what?"

"I don't know."

Didi sighed once, then resumed. "How often did you do this kind of thing for him?"

"Every month."

"And how many checks are we talking about?"

"Three a month. Eight-eight dollars per check."

"Exactly that amount—eighty-eight dollars."

"Yes. Always."

"And were they always from the same person?"

"Well, the same *three* people."

"Who?"

He shook his head and was silent. Didi didn't know what to ask next. This was an unexpected development—an utterly bizarre one.

Now it was Rose who tightened the noose. "Harland," she said breathlessly, "what if one of those check writers killed Wynton?"

"Don't be stupid," he said testily.

Didi leaped back in. "Then you know their names! If you're that sure, you know those three people."

The game was lost. Harland Frick spoke slowly, barely audible: "Robert Lorenz, Willy Prosper, and Cynthia Bracken."

They were all locals. Two dairy farmers and a healer. It made as much sense to Didi as if they were two pig farmers and a chiropractor. Or two astronauts and a disc jockey.

"And you still say you don't know what the money was for, Harland?"

"That's right. I don't know."

"Do you have anything else to tell us?"

"No."

"Did Wynton Chung store any of his personal possessions with you? Papers? Anything?"

Harland smirked for a long moment before answering sarcastically, "No. Shopkeeper Frick has told state troopers Nightingale and Vigdor all he knows. The confession will stand up in court."

As Didi left, she wondered why she had not asked the old man about the dappled colt. If there ever had been wild horses in Hillsbrook, they would have entered the folklore. And that was Harland's milieu. But she kept on walking.

Chapter 6

Trent Tucker and Abigail entered the kitchen together. The breakfast table was set. Trent looked out of the window. The Boss was doing her breathing exercises outside in the chill morning.

He sat down in his usual spot, Abigail in hers.

But something was wrong. Mrs. Tunney's disconsolate look was plain to see. She was making no move toward the oatmeal on the stove.

And Charlie was nowhere to be seen.

"Where's Charlie?" Trent inquired.

The old lady Tunney waved her hands as if to say she knew the answer but it would be impossible to explain.

"Is he sick?" Trent asked.

"Not sick the way you mean," she said wearily. And she leaned over and spoke in a whisper to the assembled: "He was already in the kitchen when I came in this morning. Do you know what he was doing? Setting the table! Can you imagine it? Charlie Gravis has never set a table in his life. He never does a darn thing he doesn't have to do.

"But there he was, bright and early, setting the table. And then he turns around and asks me if there's anything else I'd like him to do. Can you believe it? 'No, Charlie,' I say to him. 'Just you sit down and wait for the others.' But he says he won't be taking regular meals with us anymore. He'll be eating only when he's hungry, he says, and then only a few scraps at that. A few scraps! Then out he walks with this crazy look on his face. Out he walks."

She folded her arms and waited for the collective response to her tale.

Abigail said nothing, however. She sat silently twirling her spoon.

Trent Tucker only mumbled "You betta tell the doc."

"Oh no!" Mrs. Tunney said quickly. "I can't mention this to Miss Quinn!"

"Why not?" Trent said. "If he's acting crazy like that, it may be dangerous. He may have a blood clot or something traveling up to his head. I heard about those things."

"You don't understand. Miss Quinn may be looking to get rid of Charlie as her veterinary assistant and get that young friend of hers in the job—that Rose girl. If something is really the matter with Charlie it'd be her chance to give him the boot. I mean, God bless our Miss Quinn. She wouldn't hurt any of us, but—"

"Okay, okay, forget it. Forget the blood clot. Maybe he's just in the middle of one of his get-rich-quick things—the lottery, horses, whatever. Who knows? Maybe he's thinking of all that cash rolling in, so he starts acting strange in the real world."

Having delivered what he considered a long enough and intelligent enough exposition, Trent Tucker took a quick glance at the oatmeal on the stove and then gave Mrs. Tunney a pleading look. He was hungry.

But Mrs. Tunney was still in a form of post-Charlie Gravis-setting-the-breakfast-table shock. Trent looked at Abigail for support in his silent plea for breakfast. Maybe she would start the damn ball rolling so they could eat and get out of the kitchen and get on with the day.

What he saw was disturbing. Abigail had one of those strange expressions on her face—no doubt, some internal music going on. Guitars in her head. And that eyes cast downward look and the nervous little flick of the tongue to the sides of her mouth. Yes, Abigail was guarding a secret. But whose secret?

"What's going on with you, Abby? You know something about old man Gravis?"

Abigail nodded shyly.

Mrs. Tunney came alive again. "Well, speak up, girl."

Abigail did, in her usual flat, quiet voice, not looking at the other two, one hand playing with her golden hair, twisting it the way a little girl might, though she was twenty-four.

"Last night, after I had finished tying up the yard dogs and giving them a treat and saying good night to them and singing them an old Leonard Cohen song—you know how they like that one about Jesus being a sailor—well, then I went to the barn to tuck in Promise Me. And there was Charlie."

"With the horse?" an astonished Mrs. Tunney asked.

"Oh no. He was with the pigs. He was sitting in Sara's pen."

"Oh my Lord," Mrs. Tunney said, clutching at the neckline of her dress. "He was just sitting there in the pigpen?"

"No, not exactly just sitting. He had this funny little book in his hands. And he was reading the book . . . to Sara. He must have heard me, but he didn't even turn his head. He just kept reading."

There was a long silence as the three elves tried to decipher this very disturbing report.

Alas, no analysis was forthcoming, so, at last, Mrs. Tunney simply announced: "We have trouble."

Then she began to dole out the oatmeal.

Usually, after her morning exercise and a cup of coffee, Dr. Nightingale showered.

But this morning, the moment she climbed the stairs up to her bedroom, she drank only half a cup, foregoing the shower, and dialed Art Moldava's number in Cooperstown. It was not yet 6:30 A.M.

Allie picked up the phone. It was obvious she had awakened him. She apologized. He said not to bother.

"I spoke to the motel clerk," she reported.

"And?" His voice was clipped and full of anxiety.

"Nothing. He claims the motel doesn't store or keep anything for guests. Ruth Stringfellow wouldn't help me either."

"What does she have to do with anything?"

"It seems Wynton Chung was sleeping with her as well as Rose."

"That's hard to believe."

"She denies it, Allie. But it's the truth. She was a frequent visitor to his room." Didi paused. She didn't want to drop the next thing on him if he was still out of control.

"Are you okay?"

"I'm fine!" he fairly shouted.

"Good. I did find out something else, something very strange."

"What?"

"Harland Frick was cashing checks every month for Chung."

"Checks? What do you mean?"

"He was getting eighty-eight dollars a month from three separate people."

"What people?"

"Robert Lorenz, Willy Prosper, and Cynthia Bracken."

"For what?"

"Harland claims he doesn't know."

"Who is this Willy Prosper? I heard of the other two."

"Prosper's a dairy farmer near Dover Plains."

There was silence on the other end. Didi knew he was squirming. Any way one looked at this thing . . . any way one turned it around . . . one had to come to the conclusion that Wynton Chung was doing something he shouldn't have been doing. No matter the pathetically small amount of the checks, or their source.

"Allie!" she called into the receiver. No response. She could hear him light a cigarette, inhale deeply.

A therapeutic move seemed called for. Didi decided to change the subject. "Did you see the psychiatrist yet?" she asked.

He did not answer. "Talk to them, Didi," he said instead. His voice was now so leaden and sad that tears sprang to her eyes.

"Do you want me to come out there, Allie? I'll come out there and stay with you. I'll take a few days off. We could—"

"Talk to them, Didi," he repeated, interrupting her.

"All right. I will. But listen to me—"

He didn't listen, though. He just said, "Love you," and hung up.

Didi sat on the edge of the bed cradling the coffee cup in both hands, rocking slightly.

She stared down into the lukewarm liquid. Yes, she would go and interview all three of the people who were making monthly payments to Wynton Chung. She'd leave a note for Charlie to man the phones in the clinic. She'd do the Lorenz and Prosper visits on her own. And she'd ask Rose to accompany her to the home of Cynthia Bracken, who lived with her sister. It would be better that way. Didi had heard that the sisters did not like professional, university-trained veterinarians.

The plan was good, the contours clearly mapped out. But she did not get up just yet. A feeling of inexplicable dread had invaded her. Well, no, it was different from dread—more a fear of loss. Like when her mother was dying. It did not make sense. The worst had already happened. She would miss Chung but not in the way she missed her mother. Or was this about some future loss? Allie? Who?

I have to start moving, she thought. Yet she sat there, rooted to the bed.

Then she put the cup down on the small end table and lay back. This was her mother's bed, in what had been her mother's room. I'm acting like a nine-year-old, she thought, not a twenty-nine-year-old. She closed her eyes. The dread was easing. She remembered what her mother used to do when she was depressed: no alcohol; no music. No. She would take out the postcard she had bought in a museum during a trip to the big city. It was a reproduction of a painting by the French artist Marc Chagall. Two dancing cows, one of them fiddling as she danced.

Didi laughed. She took a deep breath and got up. Then she showered, dressed, left the note for Charlie, made the call to Rose, and hit the road in her red Jeep.

She found Robert Lorenz in his dairy barn, measuring out feed with a scoop.

The moment she walked through the door and he laid eyes on her, he began to talk: "I haven't got the bill yet. I'll pay it when I get it."

"I'm not here to collect a fee," Didi said.

"Well, you deserve it. I coat the rail with junk. The filly doesn't go near it. And her eyes are fine. So send me your bill and I'll be happy to pay it."

"She's a lovely little filly," Didi said. It was a horsewoman's cliché and the big farmer thrust his scoop into the feed bin and stared at her. The gaze said "get down to business, lady. I work for a living."

She blurted out the name Wynton Chung.

Lorenz picked up the scoop again and studied it with an academic air.

"You know that name, Mr. Lorenz?"

"Don't everyone who reads the papers know that name?"

"But not everyone gave him money—like you did."

"Me?"

"Yes, every month. A check for exactly eighty-eight dollars."

"What if I did?"

"I want to know why."

"You do, do you? Well, I may *want* to throw you off my property. I may *want* a strawberry short-cake for lunch. What we want and what we get, Miss Veterinarian, are two different things sometimes."

"Mr. Lorenz, if you gave him money each month for something legitimate, I don't understand why you wouldn't be quite willing to tell me what it was for. After all, what is there to hide?"

"Tell me, is the vet business that bad these days? Is that it? The cows vanishing and there ain't enough arthritic poodles to go around? Are you a bank investigator in your spare time? Is the bank really worried about my lousy eighty-eight-buck checks? Oh yeah, I got it. Drug money. Like on TV. Everything is drug money. Well, I confess. I give up, okay? I was using Wynton Chung to launder drug money. The cows in this barn produce cocaine raw milk. And it goes from here right into the orphan's home."

She thought it best not to respond to the nasty outburst. She just lounged there, staring down at her boots.

"Okay," Lorenz said in a minute.

She looked up.

"Okay okay okay! It wasn't anything, really. You're way off base if you think there was anything crooked going on. Do you remember those barn fires about eight years ago? Here?"

"Eight years ago I was away at school."

"Oh. Well, see, kids were driving through Hillsbrook throwing beer cans and Molotov cocktails at cows in the pastures. When the cans missed? No problem. When the Molotov cocktails missed they sometimes lit up a barn. You know, fool drunk kids."

"I've never heard of anything like that happening recently, Mr. Lorenz."

"It hasn't," he quickly agreed. "But it will sooner or later—and you just can't be too careful."

"What are you saying?"

"I'm saying what I'm saying. I paid Chung to keep a watch on this place. To drive by at night, check it out. You know."

"Are you telling me he was your fire marshal?"

"If it has a tail, two ears, moos, and gives milk—it may well be a cow, missy."

"I see. And did Chung ever—"

"No more, Miss Nightingale," he stopped her question before she could phrase it. "No more!" Lorenz was angry now, really angry.

Didi thanked him with excessive if insincere politeness and left his property.

As she drove toward Dover Plains, she felt blank and uncomfortable. Lorenz had given her a simple, logical explanation. And considering the perpetual paranoia of dairy farmers, she believed him. If what Robert Lorenz said was true, then

Chung's reputation as an exemplary police officer was still intact—providing, of course, that he was off duty when he was acting as fire marshal.

Suddenly, furiously, she realized what a fool she was to be thinking about reputation at a time like this. No matter what his reputation, the man had been shot dead. Destroyed.

Willy Prosper was a kindly, jovial young farmer with an impressive operation. Of course, he was the last working dairy farmer in the area, so comparisons were difficult.

When she introduced herself he cocked his head, his shock of brown hair falling over his eyes, and said, "You know, I believe I have heard of you. I mean, I've heard of this real pretty young vet in the Hillsbrook area who knows her stuff. I guess you must be her."

Didi laughed appreciatively. Compliments aside, she liked this man. She liked the way he spoke and the way he looked—sturdy cross-strapped coveralls over a thick denim shirt, a red and black bandanna covering his head, huge, ugly brown boots coated with layers of mud. He already had the dairyman's stoop, though he couldn't have been more than thirty-five.

She realized on closer inspection that his hair was auburn, not brown, and his face was pleasingly freckled.

"I am she," Didi said, "or at least I hope I am."

"That's a shame, Doctor Nightingale," he said with a mischievous smile, "because my stock is all healthy at the moment. But I promise the next time they come down with anything, I'll call you and you can come to see us . . . if not before then."

Ah. A little country flirting, Didi thought, frankly enjoying it.

"Well, I'd be happy to, Mr. Prosper. But I'm not here on veterinary business now."

He had been leaning on one of the storage sheds that abutted the dairy barn. Now he squatted, massaging his left knee. At Didi's curious look, he explained, "Early onset arthritis, the doctor told me."

From within the barn came the sound of bellowing cows. It was a lovely, deep, resonant sound, like bass bells in some cathedral.

"They're getting mad," Prosper said. "I was just about to turn them out when you came."

It was the dairy farmer's polite way of asking her to get to the point. But she hesitated. She didn't want to elicit the kind of hostility that Robert Lorenz had shown with his babbling about bank examiners.

"I was a friend of Wynton Chung's," she said, and then decided to rely on an old saw that seemed to mean everything and nothing: "We're trying to get his affairs in order."

He jumped right in. "And you found out about my payments to him—right? You want to know if any other money is owed to the estate—right? Hell, I can understand that."

Then his expression saddened and he added,

"You know, I didn't see him much, but I really liked him."

"What were those payments for, Mr. Prosper?"

"Call me Willy," he interjected. Then he pointed north toward a heavily wooded slope. "Do you see those woods?"

"I see them."

"A whole lot of deer in there. And it attracts a whole lot of dogs running loose. About a year ago some of those dogs chased a deer on to my property. They forgot the deer quick enough when they saw two calves. One they killed right out. The other one got chewed up real bad."

"And what does this have to do with Wynton? What, specifically, did he do for his fee?"

"He would take a run by those woods from time to time. If he saw feral dogs he'd get them out of there one way or the other. Or he'd tell me and I'd do the job. Usually it was me."

There was nothing further to say. Didi thanked him and returned to her Jeep. This was turning out to be a pathetic goose chase. The reasons for the payments were becoming more and more mundane.

She drove to Rose Vigdor's place and the two of them headed toward the Bracken sisters' home. Didi filled Rose in on her visits to Lorenz and Prosper.

"So those checks didn't mean a thing," Rose said. "And to think we almost had to beat it out of poor old Harland."

"Yes, we really sweated old Harland. But it was probably his reluctance that made us suspicious."

"You know, Didi, it would have been very bad if poor Wynton had been a crooked cop."

"Amen to that."

"Maybe we should forget about the Brackens."

"Let's just finish what we started, Rose. It'll only take a few minutes."

They pulled onto the dirt road that led to the Bracken place. It was a big old clapboard house with a wraparound porch. The house was in disrepair. But just past the house was row upon row of raised garden beds, meticulously laid out and cared for.

Didi turned off the ignition.

"They're serious gardeners," said Rose, sounding almost awestruck.

"Looks like medicinal herbs for the most part," speculated Didi, "and a few vegetables for the pot."

"Which sister is which?" Rose asked, nodding at the women.

Didi stared at the two women busy in the garden, surrounded by wheelbarrows, spades, and sheets of black plastic. The sisters were in their mid-forties and they looked very much alike. In fact there was only a year difference in their ages. Both were dressed in auto-mechanic-type overalls and high boots with thick sponge soles. One of them wore a beret and the other had a long blue

muffler knotted tightly at her throat, the ends
flung back over her shoulders.

"I think the one with the hat is Louise," Didi
said.

They left the Jeep and tentatively approached
the sisters. They stopped about twenty feet away
from the older women.

"Hello," Didi called out.

The sisters looked up at the same time.

"I know you!" a wide-eyed Louise, the one in
the beret, pronounced. Cynthia immediately
turned her attention back to her gardening.

"I'm Deirdre Nightingale and this is my friend
Rose Vigdor."

"Yes!" Louise exclaimed, "you're that new vet."

"Not really new," Didi replied, laughing.

"New . . . young . . . a spring chicken . . . all the
same," Louise cackled.

"You have a beautiful garden here," Rose said.

"We don't garden for beauty," Louise said, her
voice taking on a nasty edge.

Didi had the feeling they weren't welcome. It
would be best to state the case quickly, she reasoned.

She moved closer to the other women, Rose at
her side.

"You're Cynthia Bracken, aren't you?" Didi inquired of the silent one.

There was no response. Louise began to guffaw,
making Didi uneasy. The two sisters were going to

live up to their reputation for being difficult. That was for sure.

"Miss Bracken, I'm one of the executors of Wynton Chung's estate," Didi lied. "We found that you had been paying him eighty-eight dollars every month. Can you please explain the payments?"

"Well, he wouldn't take any produce," Louise said cryptically.

Cynthia finally stood up and flung her trowel into the earth like a knife. She had a handsome, lined face and was buxom in the extreme.

"Roundworm in pigs!" she exclaimed.

"What was that?" asked Didi.

"I said, roundworm in pigs!"

Rose and Didi exchanged glances.

"What about roundworm in pigs?" asked Didi.

"You see much of it lately?"

"Some."

"How do you treat it, little girl?"

Uh-oh, Didi thought. Here we go. Again. The animosity of the herbalist for the dispenser of pharmaceuticals. The scorn of the medicine man—or woman—for the surgeon. The contempt of the astrologist for the astronomer. Well, there was no way she would take part in that kind of argument, the kind that had been going on for at least a thousand years. She really didn't care how Cynthia Bracken treated roundworm in pigs, as long as the treatment worked without killing the patient.

"Please," Didi pleaded, "just answer the question. I'm in a hurry."

Wrong strategy. Her words infuriated Cynthia Bracken, who shouted: "So are the pigs!"

Louise took three steps toward Didi, as if to shield her from a possible attack by her sister. "He weeded our garden a couple of times a month. Sometimes he chopped wood for us. Now get into that silly red car of yours and leave us."

There seemed nothing further to say. Didi and Rose walked quickly back to the vehicle and drove off.

"That Cynthia Bracken is nuts," Rose said bitterly. "And it's so sad. She was so aggressive with you I didn't even get the chance to talk to the two of them about herbal teas for Aretha, or cornstarch compresses, and a hundred other things I wanted to discuss."

"Life can be harsh," Didi quipped, trying to keep up a brave, flippant front. But she too had been rattled by Cynthia.

"And I'll tell you something even sadder, girlfriend: poor Wynton weeding that garden and doing chores for a lousy eighty-eight bucks a month. It means he was very hard up. He must have needed money real bad."

"Agreed. But for what?"

"I haven't the vaguest idea. He wasn't buying me any mink stoles and long-stemmed roses, believe me. Anyway, I'm starving. Can we have lunch together?"

"No," Didi said. "I'm dropping you back at your place. Then I've got to get home, see what's happening."

They rode for a while without talking.

Finally, Rose broke the silence. "I can hear those wheels a-turning."

"What wheels?" asked Didi.

"You're thinking, Nightshade," Rose said, using one of her countless affectionate little variations on the name Nightingale. "I can always tell when you're thinking in a moving vehicle—you don't put on Patsy Cline."

"You're right. Something is bothering me."

"Like what?"

"I suddenly realized it is all so pat."

"What do you mean?"

"I mean, each of them had an explanation ready for the monthly payments to Chung. A perfectly logical, innocent explanation. Perfectly reasonable. All very rational. And all very rehearsed. Now, doesn't that bother you?"

"I see what you mean. Kind of like a pregnancy that goes absolutely splendid for the first eight months. In the ninth month you've got to get a little nervous. Like that?"

"Something like that."

"I don't know what to tell you, Didi. But, to be honest, after thinking about it now . . . and after making love with Wynton . . . it seems unbelievable to me that he'd hire himself out for eighty-eight dollars as a fire warden, a dogcatcher, and a weed puller. Even eighty-eight times three."

"My thoughts exactly," Didi echoed.

Charlie entered the stand of white pine. It was one of the largest such stands left in Dutchess County and the boss' mother, Faith Quinn Nightingale, had treasured it all her life.

Actually Charlie had not been in these woods more than two or three times in all the years he had lived at the Nightingale place. He wasn't a big one for sylvan settings. And to get to this stand of pine you had to go past the barn and through two overgrown fields. So Charlie, who was never a walker, had stayed out.

But now he was in that lush and beautiful and peaceful place and it was indescribably lovely. Particularly the forest floor, which seemed to have become a carpet thick with the past summer's residue and the harbingers of fall. It was like walking through a sweet-smelling cow pasture on the morning after a herd had grazed there.

He couldn't tarry too long admiring the various elements, though, because he was there for a reason—a very specific reason.

It was obvious to him that he had experienced a sudden enlightenment in the Buddhist sense . . . that he now perceived all the Noble Truths . . . and that he had to test the validity of that enlightenment in the swift-running stream at the north end of the pine woods.

He was going to peer into the stream and "see nothing." A regular old room mirror just wouldn't do the trick.

Charlie did think it odd that he had achieved this enlightened state so quickly—in only a few days' time, after reading just one book. But he had read in the same book that there were Zen sects within Buddhism that preached *sudden* enlightenment.

So, enlightenment had come to him in minimum time with a minimum of effort. So what? What the hell? It was all one big enchilada.

Now where was that stream?

He kept walking. My, but he felt good. This enlightenment stuff was incredible. Nothing and no one seemed to bother him anymore. It was like living in a newly painted world where he was forty years old again. Everything and everyone was his brother. Sometimes he even felt like addressing them not as brother but as "beloved random pattern of phenomena who just happens temporarily to be arranged a little different from me." He was the same as the squirrel and the pinecone. All impermanent, all sorrowful, all without a real self.

Now he knew where he was and could hear the stream. He walked quickly toward the sound. But he paused when he saw a particularly fine pinecone on the ground. He knelt beside it and whispered the Noble Truth to it. Then he stood up. It was amazing how limber he had become.

The stream was where it had always been, gushing suddenly out of a shallow rock basin and then running about two hundred yards to the outer edge of the stand, where it dived into the earth again.

He approached it slowly. He felt humble but a bit excited. He straddled the narrow stream and peered downward. What an amazement! There was no face staring up at him from the clear water. No Charlie Gravis. He saw nothing. Well, not exactly nothing. But the reflection was so amorphous, so distorted, that it could be considered as nothing.

Relieved, vindicated, anxious to proceed, he sat down on a rock and pulled from his back pocket Lady Barraclough's Buddhist enlightenment manual, *Look in the Mirror and See Nothing.* He was now ready for the next step. He would now become a Bodhisattva and lead Diane to the other shore—Nibbana.

He consulted the index, found the heading for Bodhisattva, and turned to the page indicated. There he found the list of the ten defining marks of a Bodhisattva.

Suddenly, from the trees above, he heard the sound of crows cawing. Yes, thought Charlie, all the signs and omens are now positive. For hadn't it been the hawk and the crows and the woodchuck that'd guided him to sudden enlightenment?

He read the list carefully.

1. The Bodhisattva vows to dedicate himself to the liberation of others. He postpones his own total extinction until all beings are free from suffering.
2. He develops sublime patience and endures all adversities.
3. He perfects discipline.
4. He burns the remnants of false ideas.
5. He grasps intuitively . . . by any mental means possible . . . the true nature of existence and craving.
6. He never forgets that he is an illusory being in a merely phenomenal world.
7. He is no longer tied to his physical body.
8. He transfers his karmic merit to unliberated beings.
9. His mind begins to radiate outward.
10. He sits on a lotus.

Charlie didn't understand what that last one was about at all. But the other nine seemed easy enough to do, now that he was enlightened.

There was a problem, however. It was important that Diane Riggins find him and recognize him for what he was now. That was essential. The truth would have to radiate out of him and into her without any persuading by him. This wasn't about selling.

He had an idea where she would find him. But how could she be sure? What were the outward signs that would lead her to say, "Behold! That nice old Charlie Gravis is really a Bodhisattva"?

Charlie thought about it a long time. It would have to be something visual—a powerful visual clue—like a cow with a full udder.

He turned to the section in Lady Barraclough's book on the life of Gotama Buddha and found the place where the possessions of the enlightened one were detailed:

three robes; alms bowl; razor; needle; a girdle; and a water strainer.

Charlie, now himself an enlightened one, found this list eminently sensible.

There were two ways for Didi to drive home from Rose Vigdor's place. The longer way, on county roads, was really the easiest. The shorter way had a lot of dirt roads. She chose the latter because she was thinking about those eighty-eight dollar checks and Allie and the Bracken sisters and a whole lot of other things; and when she was engaged in that kind of thinking she liked to put the Jeep through its paces.

As she drove, sifting through all the recent events, it was the Bracken sisters she fastened on with the highest concentration. What made those two so downright nasty? What had she done to them? She surely was no rival, no competitor to them. The only person she had ever met who had first used them to treat his animals and then called her in was Robert Lorenz. Unless . . . unless there were many people who employed the Brackens rather than traditional vets but for their own reasons just didn't broadcast it—or admit it. This, she thought, was a possibility. Hillsbrook people were sometimes a strange lot.

It was while she was chewing on this possibility and negotiating the Jeep through a series of turns that she saw the dappled colt again. At least, she *thought* she saw it—again.

No near collision this time. She braked, pulled the Jeep over, and shut the engine.

She wondered for a moment if she was going around the bend. Like Allie. Was the dappled colt merely a symptom of her oncoming madness?

Dr. Nightingale adjusted the rearview mirror carefully so that she could see the side of the dirt road, the side with trees.

She felt suddenly giddy as the colt came into full view. He was standing calmly in a clump of trees, looking reflective, as young horses tend to do.

Now, she told herself, now there can be no denying the situation. It doesn't matter who says there are no wild horses in Hillsbrook. She was looking at one. She was seeing it with her own eyes. Beyond any shadow of a doubt she was looking at a handsome gray dappled colt among the trees, no rider or halter visible. He was a thoroughbred, close to racing age. Or maybe bred for the show ring. Gosh, he was a fine lined boy, except he was a bit thin.

Oh, for a few cubes of sugar or an apple. But she had nothing like that.

She did have a sturdy rope, though, coiled in the backseat. Didi put the emergency brake on because she had parked on a rather treacherous incline. She grabbed the rope and headed for Mr. Dappled on foot. She walked slowly, and as she walked she fashioned a lariat at one end of the rope. Yes, she would gather this silly colt in before he got hurt.

During her tomboy phase—or one of them—she had decided to run away to Wyoming and join a rodeo. To that end she had taught herself how to make and throw a lariat. All those poor chickens she lassoed! They never forgave her. The phase passed, but not the skill.

Mr. Dappled calmly, curiously watched her approach, his ears forward. She walked steadily toward him, but when she was just within lariat range, the colt loped off. He put about twenty yards between them, stopped, turned, and gave Didi an assessing look accompanied by a snort.

"Now, Dappy," she crooned, "let's not be difficult."

But the scenario kept repeating: she closing ground, he trotting off.

They were moving up a brush-filled ridge. Didi was tiring but she kept at it. These kinds of pursuits required discipline and patience.

When they reached the ridgeline, the dappled colt started moving toward the east. It didn't really matter—the sun was overhead now. Didi's clothes were soaked through with sweat in spite of the coolness of the day. She realized they were now traversing the back of the Stringfellow and Fox properties; she could see the houses, barns, and fences in the distance. Maybe, she thought, Dappy had been around here before; maybe it was he who had kicked down that fence.

Then the colt slipped from sight in the high brush. One second he was in view, and the next he was gone. She stopped and twisted. Obviously he had blended in with the terrain. His coat gave him a good camouflage net. As she waited for him to reappear, she moved the loop of the lariat back and forth like a contestant in a steer-roping event waiting for the animal to be released from the pen.

A shot rang out.

There was no question. She heard a shot.

It paralyzed her with fear. Had someone shot the dappled colt? Had someone mistaken him for a deer?

She flinched when she heard the second shot.

Then the colt burst out of a clump of young willows, only ten feet away from her.

No! That wasn't the colt!

It was a thin black woman. She was staggering. And then she fell forward, hard.

Didi rushed to her. There was a great gaping,

bloody hole in the woman's back where the bullets had entered.

Didi ripped off her jacket and pressed it down on the wound to slow the bleeding.

I know her, Didi thought. I've seen this woman before—somewhere.

The victim was choking. Didi turned her partially, with great care. She looked intently at the woman's face.

It was the piano player from the Artichoke. The restaurant where she and Allie and Wynton had dined on the night Chung was murdered. This was the woman pianist who had set them dancing.

Her tongue, Didi thought, she must be swallowing her tongue. The victim, panicked, resisted her help. Didi pressed the woman's jaws, forcing her to open her mouth. Then she reached inside.

No, it wasn't the tongue. There was a wad of paper in the woman's mouth. She had been trying to swallow paper. Didi pulled the wad out and thrust it into her own shirt pocket.

The woman's eyes were open now. She was in pain and babbling. Didi whispered in her ear: "Don't try to move. Stay still. I'm getting help. You'll be okay."

Didi stood up. She noticed her hands were trembling. How unprofessional! She thrust them in her pockets and tried to rationally evaluate her options.

There was a cellular phone in the Jeep. She had recently purchased two of them—one for herself and one for Rose, so that she would not be isolated in her creaky barn. So, the Jeep was one option. The other was the phone in the Stringfellow or the Fox house.

No—going to the Jeep made more sense.

She pulled the piano player's boots off and undid all her clasps and buttons. Then she rechecked the jagged wound. The bleeding had almost ceased.

A frantic whinny echoed all around. The colt was only a few yards away, violently pawing the ground.

"Get out of here!" Didi yelled, picking up the lariat and flinging it at the horse. The dappled colt reared, pounded the rope with his front hooves, and galloped off.

Didi ran down the slope to her Jeep. She didn't dial 911; she called the Hillsbrook Police dispatcher and reported the shooting. He ordered her to stay with her vehicle until the ambulance arrived, and then lead the medical response team to the victim.

She sat in the Jeep and waited. The procedure was correct, but she wanted to be with the victim . . . to help and comfort her . . . until the ambulance arrived. She was a vet, not an M.D., but she had treated many gunshot wounds in all kinds of living things.

Her hands and chest were streaked with blood. She smelled of it. And an evil chill was crawling over her.

She reached into her shirt pocket, found the wad of paper, and started to fling it out the window. But then a strange thing happened. The single wad of paper was opening up like a rose in bud. Didi watched it separate and become six thin slips of paper in her hand.

She realized they were cigarette rolling papers. The same French brand—Zig Zag—that one of her roommates used to use when she rolled marijuana cigarettes.

But there was handwriting on these—in ink, a tiny, exquisite script.

Didi spread them on the dashboard. She opened the glove compartment and pulled out Charlie Gravis's folding magnifying glass, which he kept in the vehicle to read road maps.

She ran the magnifier over the cigarette papers.

What she found was bizarre.

The papers contained the breeding pedigrees and racing charts of three mares:

Sweet and Fast
Big Lily
Harry's Darling

She leaned back in the seat and shut her eyes, almost violently. None of this rolling paper nonsense meant anything to her.

What had that lovely young piano player played that terrible night? One song, she remembered, had particularly entranced her. But she couldn't remember the title or reproduce the tune.

She opened her eyes, but all she could see was the blood pumping out of the wound in the pianist's back.

Harland Frick sat in the rear of his store removing jars of organic peanut butter from the shipping carton and pricing them.

He had completed the first dozen when he realized it was apple butter he was dealing with and not just peanut butter.

That was a depressing error. Unless, of course, by chance the apple butter was the same wholesale price as peanut butter.

In that case there was no problem at all, because the markup was the same. He began looking for the bills.

A laughing, wild-looking Burt Conyers burst into the store, interrupting his research.

The bearded, long-haired poet—many people in Hillsbrook considered him just a wino—was wearing his usual sheepskin vest and sandals.

Harland flinched a bit, fearful he was about to hear one of Conyers's poems on rural death and passion. Burt's poems were always about that stuff, none of which Harland could follow.

Conyers pointed an accusing finger at him. "You are sitting there, Frick, like a dead wildflower. But just down the block the world is bursting open."

"What are you talking about, Burt?"

"I'm telling you that the whole town is going insane. Take a look, man!"

He swung the door open in a grand gesture. Harland followed him outside.

Yes. Something was happening. A small crowd had gathered in front of the bank, just across the street from the war memorial with its lovingly tended garden.

"Hurry, man, hurry!" Burt called, pulling at Frick's arm. "You don't want to miss this. They've wheeled the wooden horse into the heart of Troy. The city will soon fall."

Others were heading toward the bank as well. Harland noticed Ike Badian and Robert Lorenz.

Conyers pulled him around the edge of the spectator circle until they had a clearer view of what was transpiring.

"Behold the lamb of God!" Burt whispered in Harland's ear. "He is going to pull the temple down!"

Harland was getting confused by the poet's shifting imagery—from Troy to Jerusalem.

But then he forgot the imagery completely. What an incredible sight! There was Charlie Gravis standing calmly against the outside wall of the bank.

He was wearing some kind of weird kimono. Or was it one of Mrs. Tunney's bathrobes? And he was carrying a cane. His shoes were a pair of old rain rubbers and he wore no socks. In one hand he held a small mixing bowl, which he would shake from time to time to signify he was accepting alms. He was rocking slowly back and forth, his eyes half open, and there was a beatific smile on his lips.

Harland saw Ike Badian shoulder his way roughly through the onlookers until he stood directly in front of his friend.

"What the hell is going on, Charlie?" Ike demanded.

Charlie opened his eyes wide and regarded his old friend with love and compassion. But he did not respond—not verbally, anyway.

"Are you crazy, standing in the middle of town looking like that?" Badian grew more and more distraught. He looked around for help from someone among the onlookers, but no help was forthcoming.

"Let me take you home, Charlie," Ike pleaded.

No answer. Just a world of Bodhisattva compassion—a wave of love.

"If you don't want to go home you can stay at my place. But, Charlie, you have to get out of those clothes—and you gotta stop shaking that goddamn bowl!"

"I *am* hungry," admitted Charlie.

"Sure you are, Charlie. Sure you are. Come on and I'll buy you a hamburger at the diner."

Charlie smiled at Ike. Then he resumed his former posture. His declaration of hunger was merely the honesty of a Bodhisattva. He would not eat now. He was waiting for his karmic destiny in the form of Diane Riggins.

Ike began to shout then. "Do you know what is going to happen, you idiot? Men in white suits are going to come and take you away. And they'll put plugs in your ears, Charlie, and send electric shocks through you like you was no more than a toaster. Ah, I'm begging you, Charlie, come on home before it's too late."

No answer from the humble monk.

"Who the hell do you think you are?" Ike screamed at Gravis.

"I am no one," Charlie said, radiating love. "I'm nothing, Ike. I am a dead woodchuck on the road. I am the hawk who feeds on the woodchuck. I'm the crows who steal from the hawk. I am the raft that will take you to the other side."

A group of townspeople stood listening, rapt, to Charlie's confession.

There were tears in Ike Badian's voice. "Charlie, listen. Listen, boy. We'll go and get us a couple of drinks. We'll play some cards. We'll take a drive. Like old times . . . okay, Charlie? . . . Charlie?"

Robert Lorenz could stand it no more. This Gravis fellow had obviously flipped his lid. Lorenz remembered seeing the old man when Dr. Nightingale had come calling. Gravis, if he remembered, had been her veterinary assistant. The man had seemed competent and sane then. Lorenz headed toward his car. He hadn't expected such lunacy on a visit to town. Then again, he rarely came into town.

As he opened the car door and flung the two cartons of cigarettes he had purchased at the new discount drugstore onto the backseat, he heard someone call out "Bobbie!"

Lorenz turned immediately. That was what he had been called as a child. No one called him Bobbie anymore.

There was a man in a red hunting jacket standing in front of the stationery store, waving at him. The man looked vaguely familiar.

"Did you call me?" Lorenz asked loudly, a little belligerent.

The fellow laughed and simply called out the name again: "Bobbie." Then he walked into the alley between the stationery store and the post office.

Robert Lorenz followed, angry now, calling out as he walked, "Hey! Hey you! Who are you?"

These were the last words he ever spoke. The moment he turned into the alley, a bullet from a .44 caliber handgun ripped into his stomach, slamming him into the wall. A second bullet tore into his Adam's apple.

A few seconds later he was dead.

Chapter 7

Dr. Deirdre Quinn Nightingale lay on her bed in the dark, still clothed in her bloody shirt and jeans.

She was exhausted, frightened, dazed.

It had been a day unlike any other in the memory of the citizens of Hillsbrook.

A woman was shot at noon. She now lay in a coma. A dairy farmer was shot dead in the afternoon, right in the middle of town. The weapon in both cases appeared to be a .44 caliber pistol.

These events combined with the recent murder of police officer Wynton Chung to make the bucolic town of Hillsbrook the undisputed murder capital of Dutchess County, New York.

There was further confusion in the Nightingale household. Charlie Gravis had vanished after his bizarre behavior—begging in the town square clothed in what a near-hysterical Mrs. Tunney referred to as pajamas.

From where she lay, even at this hour, Didi could still hear her elves in the kitchen. They didn't know what to do, where to find Charlie, or what had deranged him.

On the bed beside her lay the six cigarette rolling papers on which were written the pedigrees and racing charts.

These ridiculous items had capped the horrendous day. She had called a knowledgeable horsewoman, a former trainer at the Finger Lakes Race Track, Pearl Gaulton.

Pearl had heard of all the mares listed: Sweet and Fast, Big Lily, Harry's Darling. All three had raced well, she said, at various tracks in the Northeast. In the mid-1970s! And all three horses were, to the best of her knowledge, dead.

The problem was, the dates on the cigarette papers indicated that these mares were still alive and had just finished their racing careers.

It was inexplicable, almost as inexplicable as the fact that someone would make the effort to write on cigarette rolling papers, copying the original records faithfully except for bogus dates . . . and almost as inexplicable as the fact that the piano player, whose name was Tai Draper, according to police, would try to swallow them.

Yes, it had been quite a day, and it had all started with that dappled colt.

She knew she should phone Allie. No doubt he already knew about the new shootings; it was all over the news. But what was she going to say to him? About anything? Tell him the payments to Chung by Lorenz, Prosper, and Bracken had seemed trivial and clean? Who cared? Things were spinning out of control. People were spinning out of reach.

As for Charlie Gravis, she felt miserable about him. Why hadn't she sensed that something was wrong with him? After all, she worked with the man every day. Why hadn't she been able to see and ease whatever torment he was going through?

Didi lay in the darkened room on her back, staring at the ceiling, wishing for sleep, praying for it. The world of Hillsbrook was too much with her.

But it was not until one in the morning that she fell asleep.

And she was awakened just forty minutes later by the jangling phone beside her bed.

Didi had been in such a deep sleep and the phone had given her such a start that for a brief moment she found herself sitting on the edge of the mattress, holding the receiver she had just picked up, but unable to figure out where she was.

It was Rose on the other end of the line.

"Isn't it the middle of the night?" Didi asked, confused.

"Yes. But never mind that. You have to come over here."

"Why?"

Didi was fully awake now. The stench of old blood on her clothing reached her nostrils. She held the receiver up to her ear with one hand and with the other began to unbutton and remove her dirty shirt.

"Someone's here to see you," Rose said.

There was an edge to Rose's voice that Didi found disturbing.

"Rose, what's the matter with you? Who's there? Who is it that wants to see me?"

"Just get over here."

"Now?"

"Yes, now. Right now."

This day will never be over, Didi thought. Never. "Is it the dogs, Rose? Is one of them sick or hurt?"

Rose's voice became clipped and angry. "Who mentioned anything about a dog? What's the matter with you, Night Gown? Wake up and smell the coffee. I told you someone is here to see you."

"Hostage!" Didi shouted into the phone. "Is someone holding you hostage?"

The question was only half in jest. It didn't matter. Rose hung up.

Didi showered and dressed at a rapid pace, then ran lightly down the stairs.

At the foot of the staircase her elves—Mrs. Tunney, Abigail, and Trent Tucker—waited in ambush for her.

"Why aren't you people sleeping?"

Mrs. Tunney explained, "We were in the kitchen, miss. We heard the phone and thought maybe it was Charlie."

"Well, it wasn't," Didi said. "And there's no reason to believe something bad has happened to him. Maybe he just got into bad company and had a few drinks and . . ."

She couldn't finish the thought. She walked right past them, into the night.

Rose was waiting for her outside the barn.

"You took your damn sweet time getting here."

"Cleanliness is next to godliness. There was stinking blood all over me."

"I'm sorry," Rose said quietly. "I forgot you went to the hospital with her. I forgot you stopped her bleeding and all."

"Did you ever notice, Rose, how I have this astonishing facility for being in the wrong place at the right time? There I was—chasing a crazy colt and—"

Rose took her by the arm and led her to the small stove in the barn.

A nervous and pale Harland Frick sat next to the heat source on a folding chair. The moment he saw Didi come in, he stood up.

"Thank you for coming," he said. "I didn't want to go to your place at this hour. I thought it would be best talking like this."

"What's this about, Harland?"

"I didn't tell you the complete truth when you and Rose were in the store the other day."

"Why tell the truth now—at two in the morning?"

"Because of what is happening. Because of all these horrible killings. I mean, I don't know why

I'm so frightened but I am. And I don't know anymore what is important and what is trivial."

"You mean you didn't tell me the truth about the checks you cashed for Chung? There were other monthly payments to him?"

"No. Not that."

"Then what?"

"I'm a little uncomfortable, so bear with me. Wynton asked me to keep what I'm about to tell you a secret. He said he would appreciate my discretion in the matter."

"I'm waiting, Harland. Take your time."

"Why are you so unfriendly to Harland?" Rose interceded. "The man has come here in the middle of the night to give you information. You act as if you're the one doing him a favor."

Didi made no answer to Rose's charge. Instead, she nodded to Harland, indicating that he should continue.

He went on, "About half the cash I gave him—after he endorsed the checks over to me—he then gave to Burt Conyers to buy booze for himself and his friends. Actually, Wynton brought the cash over to the liquor store and told the counterman who to take care of. Conyers first, of course. He was trotting behind Wynton like a thirsty puppy."

"And you think this is important for me to know?" a skeptical Didi asked.

"No, I don't. But what he did with the other half of the cash may well be."

"Which was?"

"He gave it to me."

"To do what?"

"To bring a widow woman in Clinton Corners goat cheese and goat's milk a few times a month."

"What's her name?"

"Sarah Lukacs."

"Did you know her?"

"No. Do you?"

"No."

"Anyway, Wynton joked with me about it. He said I better not screw up with the deliveries because the old lady was his banker."

"Banker? What did he mean by that?"

"I have no idea, but you must admit it was a very strange term to use."

"So you made these deliveries?"

"Yes. As long as I continued cashing checks. The last one was about two weeks before he was murdered."

"Maybe Chung was just playing the Good Samaritan," Rose offered. "Booze for the alkies, health food for the widows."

"Did you talk to Sarah Lukacs when you made the deliveries?" asked Didi.

"No. Just hello and good-bye and enjoy the food."

"But she did know who was paying for it?"

"I assume."

Harland Frick rose to go.

"Nothing else?"

"Nothing else." But then a minute later he

added, "I don't know what it means. I don't know your involvement. But I figured, since you're close to Allie Voegler, you had a reason for pressing. Maybe—" He didn't finish the thought. He looked at Rose and smiled apologetically.

"Well, I appreciate your coming here," Didi said.

He slipped out of the barn quietly. A minute later the two women heard his car engine cough, roar up, and then fade away.

"Now what?" asked Rose.

"I'll call Allie in the morning. If he wants me to visit this Sarah Lukacs, I will."

"Why don't you park here for the rest of the night?"

"That makes sense. Thanks."

Didi sat down on the mat beside the stove. The dogs surrounded her. Bozo demanded to be scratched. Didi pushed him away.

"Do you think that piano player will make it, Didi?"

"I don't know. It doesn't look good."

"She was lucky you were around. Otherwise she would have either bled to death or choked to death on that ridge."

"Did I tell you what she was choking on?"

"No."

Didi proceeded to tell her friend about the pedigree and racing charts meticulously scripted on the thin sheets of rolling paper.

"Maybe she studies calligraphy," Rose said impishly.

"Maybe you're Hillary Clinton. Anyway, even if she is a calligrapher in her spare time, as a hobby say, why this kind of stuff? And why try to swallow it?"

"She was in shock. She might not have known what she was doing."

"Plausible."

"Did you know that dairy farmer who was gunned down a few hours later?"

"Yes, I knew Robert Lorenz. Not as a friend. But only a few days ago I was at his place. A filly had some eye trouble."

"Do you think the shootings were related?"

"I have no idea. They say it was the same caliber gun."

"And poor Charlie Gravis. What do you think is going on with that weird old man? Harland told me he saw Charlie doing his new routine in town. Just before that dairy farmer got killed. It was only two blocks from where Charlie was modeling his new minimalist collection."

Didi shook her head mournfully. "I have no idea what's going on with Charlie. The others are blaming his weird behavior on some book or other he's been reading. I don't know what they're talking about. Obviously, he just snapped."

Didi leaned forward to study the flame. Rose made tea and then served it with a new kind of chip—cauliflower.

Rose mused, "Who would have thought when I moved from the big city up here that pretty little

Hillsbrook would turn out to be like the South Bronx or Dodge City. Girl, I want my deposit back."

Dr. Nightingale did not find it funny at all. But then again, she was very tired. What she really did find amusing was the idea of Wynton Chung giving Harland Frick money to take goat cheese to a widow in Clinton Corners. Frick had called her a widow woman. What a charmingly old-fashioned expression. It was, however, a very subtle kind of humor. A kind of humor that had to be explicated. Maybe tomorrow.

"Mommy, tell me the story of the dappled colt wandering the countryside," Rose teased.

"What dappled colt?" Didi said, not missing a beat. "Don't you know there are no wild horses in Hillsbrook, child?"

Charlie opened his eyes. He saw the morning. And he smiled. He had slept with his back against a heated henhouse. There was no chill in his body, though there was surely one in the air.

He was hungry and there was a bit of muscle discomfort, but that was all right. His sojourn in town had been unsuccessful: no one had filled his alms bowl with bread crusts and Diane Riggins had not appeared. But that too was all right.

There were sounds all around him—from the henhouse, from the fields, from a cohort of diving birds.

The thought came to him that there must be certain procedures or rituals that Bodhisattvas perform upon rising. But Lady Barraclough had not mentioned anything specific in her ten points distinguishing Bodhisattvas. Well, the good woman had a lot to say in a small book; no doubt she had had to leave a lot out.

It made sense to preach a bit. Yes. That made sense. He pulled out his guide and turned to the appendix which contained many authentic sermons of Gotama Buddha. He picked the one applicable, in his mind, for an autumn morning behind a henhouse, turned to face the wall, and addressed the hens within, although he could not be sure they were hearing him.

Of course, where the Buddha used the term "monks" he substituted "hens." After all, he was a Bodhisattva—he had some leeway.

"I tell you, hens, that in your body, with its perception and thinking, lies all the world; the origin of the world; the cessation of the world; and the path to cessation of the world.

"Answer me, O hens! What do you think is more? All the water in the four great oceans or all the tears you have shed when wandering, lamenting, and weeping in your journey, because you received what you truly hated and did not receive what you truly loved."

He closed the book. Whew, that was a mouthful.

Another thought came to him after he had preached to the hens. Why not find Diane Riggins now rather than wait for a karmic coincidence?

After all, time was of the essence. Worlds were being formed and destroyed at an incredible rate. And she was suffering. This was the compassionate thing to do. He dusted himself off, walked through the field, and out onto the main road.

After a half hour of brisk walking, he reached the converted mansion now called the Raft. The grounds, he noticed, were manicured. The small parking lot, which had replaced a kennel that used to house foxhounds, was empty.

He strode up the steps and boldly rang the bell on the door. A tall, thin young man wearing a black suit, rose-colored shirt, and dark gray tie opened the door. He stared at Charlie in disbelief, then composed himself enough to speak a simple "Yes?"

"I am here to see Diane Riggins."

"Riggins? Was she at the retreat?"

"Yes."

"Of course. Now I remember Diane. She's gone. The retreat is over. She went back to Manhattan yesterday."

This was an unforeseen event. Charlie pondered in silence.

"Who are you?" the young man asked.

Charlie could not lie. "I am a Bodhisattva," he admitted.

"Oh really?"

"May I have her address in Manhattan?"

"I'm afraid I'm not allowed to give that information out."

"She would want me to have it."

"Oh really?" Same expression, only this time the young man could barely suppress his mirth.

Once upon a time, Charlie acknowledged, he would have become angry with this man from the Raft. But now, all he did was smile and hold out his alms bowl toward the man, who quickly stepped backward, as if the bowl would harm him. His mirth had vanished. "All I know," he said, "is that she lives at Hanover Square. Do you know downtown Manhattan?"

Charlie stared, waiting for the remainder of the instructions.

"That's somewhere between Wall Street and the South Street Seaport," the young man said.

Charlie nodded, memorizing the information.

"But tell me, who are you—really?" the young man added impulsively.

But Charlie was already on his way to Route 9, the old road that snaked south along the Hudson to the big city.

Once on the road, he positioned himself just past a gas station and waited calmly.

Cars passed him, trucks, buses—all flew by on the winding road, but no one wanted to stop for the holy man.

Then, suddenly, a huge concrete-mixer truck ground to a halt in front of him. The driver leaned over, opened the passenger door, and shouted out: "What's going on with you, Pop? It's not Halloween yet."

Charlie replied, "For suffering mankind, every day is Halloween."

"Ain't that the truth," said the driver. "Where you headed?"

"Manhattan . . . downtown."

"Hop in. I'll drop you at the Holland Tunnel."

The morning sun had quickly vanished and a light rain was now tattooing the roof of Rose's barn.

Didi dialed Art Moldava's number on Rose's cellular phone. A clipped voice answered: "Voegler here."

"It's me, Didi."

"It's about goddamn time. I've been waiting all night. Why didn't you call? What the hell is the matter with you?"

"Stop barking at me, Allie. Calm down."

"Calm down? Hillsbrook's going up in flames and I'm in Cooperstown. You know how that makes me feel? What do you want me to do—visit the Baseball Hall of Fame? It's only two blocks away. But you know me, Didi. I don't like baseball. I like blood sports—boxing, hunting, football. Isn't that what you and your friend think? Isn't that what you always thought? Allie Voegler, aka Albert J. Voegler, aka the man who likes to terrorize with gun and badge. You always knew I was going to beat up on a suspect one day, didn't you? You always knew I was going to slap a girl around, didn't you? That's the real reason we're not together anymore, isn't it?"

The outburst stopped abruptly. Didi felt no anger—only a desire to help him, to calm him, to touch him. He was running wild like the dappled colt and he needed a lariat.

There was silence. Finally she said, "I think you are a gentle, caring man. And I have always thought that, deer hunting not withstanding."

There was more silence. Cigarette lighter flicking open. Intake of breath. Then she heard him say, "Talk to me."

She reported on the visits to Lorenz, Prosper, the Bracken sisters, about their explanations of their eighty-eight dollar a month payments to Chung. She told him about the shooting of the young piano player on the ridge. And then she got around to telling him what she had been holding back: Harland Frick's revelation that Wynton Chung was giving money to winos and goat cheese to one Sarah Lukacs.

Last, the murder of Robert Lorenz in town—what little she knew of it.

Allie spoke not a word during her narrative. When it was finished he said, "You know, I cannot for the life of me remember the face of that girl piano player at the Artichoke that night. What did you say her name was again?"

"Her name is Tai Draper. What do you make of it, Allie?"

He laughed self-deprecatingly. "As Hillsbrook's

top cop in exile, I say it's either meaningful or meaningless. Anyway, tell me about this Lewis woman that Chung was helping out."

"Not Lewis. Lukacs. Sarah Lukacs. She's a widow apparently. She lives in Clinton Corners. Does that name ring a bell?"

"I don't know. Vaguely. Very vaguely."

"Harland says that Chung used to call her his banker. It was some kind of running joke. Any idea what he could have meant by that?"

"None. But it doesn't sound good. There's something kind of ugly about it, matter of fact."

"I agree. Do you think I ought to pay her a visit? I mean, is it possible she has his personal belongings? In short, shouldn't I find out who Sarah Lukacs is?"

All he said in response was, "It's cold and wet here, Didi. And I'm lonesome for you. Maybe you should come out here. I am so lonesome for you I feel like a whiskey bottle in Mrs. Tunney's bedroom."

"Now that *is* lonesome."

"I want us to start over when all this gets straightened out."

"Do you want me to go to Sarah Lukacs?"

He didn't like that she had changed the subject; that she didn't affirm his plan to start over. So he snapped, "Do what you want. You always do, anyway, Dr. Nightingale."

Why, she thought, is it always such a struggle with this man?

"I'll get back to you soon," she said, ending the call.

Rose walked into the barn holding her small transistor radio in the air like a trophy.

"The piano player is dead," she announced. "I just heard the news. She died at five o'clock in the morning in the intensive care unit. They're bringing in a special contingent of state troopers to assist the Hillsbrook police." She laughed a bit wildly. "What's next—the National Guard?"

Dr. Nightingale closed her eyes. A wave of nausea came over her. How old was Tai Draper? she thought. Where did she come from? Where did she learn to play the piano like that? What was she doing on that ridge bordering the Stringfellow and Fox properties? Why would she keep those rolling papers in her mouth like a wad of bubble gum? Why did she have to die?

Didi felt something cold and moist in her hand and jumped. It was only Aretha's nose.

"Do you know what I think, Nightingale?" Rose said.

"What?"

"I think a madman is loose."

"Different madmen. Different weapons," Didi noted. "Maybe one madman killed the girl and Lorenz. It looks like they were both killed with a .44 caliber handgun. But a hunting rifle did the Chung murder."

"No," Rose objected strenuously. "One madman in many forms."

"You're getting irrational, Rose."

"And you're getting crushed, Deirdre dear. I've seen it happening since Wynton died. You're getting squashed. You're losing your—how shall I say it?—your style. You're like a grumpy old widow woman. Maybe you need some goat cheese."

"Very funny."

"No, I mean it. You need to get ahold of yourself. You see death all the time in your practice. I don't. Besides, I was the one who slept with Wynton—not you."

"Why don't you come with me now and see a real widow woman. Then we can make comparisons."

"I'm ready. Just let me feed the dogs. And on the way over you can tell me about your latest man trouble."

"What man trouble?"

"Officer Voegler."

"Allie's under the weather."

"I'd say he's under a rock."

"Rose, I've always wondered where you got your love 'em and leave 'em philosophy."

Rose threw back her head and laughed. Then she aborted the laugh and shook her head vigorously. "I'm carrying on with false bravado," she said.

"Aren't we all?"

"The fact of the matter is, I have never been more frightened in my life. It's like a noose is tightening around the neck of Hillsbrook. Can't you feel it too? Do you know what I'm saying? And no one in this charming little burg seems to know or care who the hangman is."

"Believe me," Didi said gravely, "they do care."

Rose fed the dogs their usual steaming mess of oats, raw chopped beef, honey, chopped scallions and parsley, a little yogurt, and God knows what else.

The drive to Clinton Corners did not take long. The Lukacs' house was a tiny country gem set far back off the road. It seemed to have been plunked down on what was once a dairy farm. Around it was the characteristic new growth woods that appear in abandoned cow pastures. The burned-out hulk of a barn sat about two hundred yards from the house.

"Will you look at those lovely red shutters?" Rose crooned. The rain cascaded down the painted wooden shutters, giving them an eerie sheen.

Didi parked the Jeep as close as possible to the house, then the two women made a dash for the door. There was no overhang to shield them from the rain. And there was no doorbell, only an old brass knocker.

Sarah Lukacs responded promptly, both her ruffled apron and her smile perfectly in place.

"I wasn't expecting visitors," she said, "but, whoever you are, you had better come in out of that rain."

She ushered them into a small hallway, duck prints on the wall. The fat porcelain umbrella stand was stuffed with oversize umbrellas as well as dainty parasols.

"You girls can borrow one if you promise to bring it back," she said.

Sarah Lukacs was a small-boned woman with short auburn hair streaked with white. She looked like a bright-eyed busy bird.

"Now, what can I do for you girls?" she asked exuberantly.

"We're sorry to barge in like this, Mrs. Lukacs, but this is important. We've come about Wynton Chung."

"Yes, that poor young man!" she said sadly, but then her expression changed to one of sudden understanding. "Oh, I see. Mr. Voegler sent you."

The statement rocked Didi. She looked quickly at Rose, then back to Mrs. Lukacs, who took the silence as an affirmation.

"It's about time he sent someone out here. I've been trying to contact him since I heard what happened to poor Wynton. They keep telling me that he's not around. 'Not around'? How can a police officer not be around?"

"Why did you want to speak to Mr. Voegler?" Didi pressed gently.

"Well, I never met the man, of course, but Wynton told me that if anything ever happened to him I was to get the bag to Mr. Voegler. You wait right here."

She vanished into the main part of the house.

"Pay dirt!" said Didi under her breath.

Rose replied in a whisper, "A fair exchange. Goat cheese for storage space."

When Sarah Lukacs returned she was dragging a heavy mountain backpack. It looked full to bursting.

"Now, you girls be sure and tell Mr. Voegler that I did try to contact him."

"Don't worry. I shall."

Didi and Rose each grabbed a strap, thanked Sarah Lukacs profusely, and dragged the pack to the Jeep.

Mrs. Lukacs stood just inside the door waving until they drove away.

The bag lay like a corpse under the front seat.

Detective Voegler presented his appointment card to the receptionist at the psychiatric wing of Bassett Hospital. She studied it, made a call, and then directed him to an office on the second floor.

He waited five minutes and was ushered into the office of Dr. C. C. Green. The first C stood for Carlotta. It made him uncomfortable that the shrink behind the desk was female.

A chunky woman with long brown hair pulled back into a fat braid, the doctor wore a wine-colored suit. She could easily pass for thirty, but Allie figured she had to be older. Her desk was bare except for one legal size yellow pad and a few ballpoint pens. She was swiveling slightly in her big leather chair.

Behind her on the wall were three small watercolors—all seascapes, one with a lighthouse in the distance.

"Do you know why you're here, Officer Voegler? Or do you prefer to be called Detective Voegler?"

"Suit yourself. I'm here because I smacked a girl in an interrogation room."

"And do you know why I'm here?"

"To make sure it doesn't happen again."

Dr. Green smiled. "Let me explain the situation. I am here to evaluate you. Not, I repeat, not, to treat you. At the end of seven or eight sessions I will write a report and that report will contain a recommendation. Only three are possible. One, you can go safely back to active duty immediately. Two, you can return to active duty but it must be in conjunction with regular visits to a therapist. Three, you cannot return to work until there is significant improvement in your psychological functioning. Do you understand?"

"It's clear," Allie said. He stared past her to the watercolor with the lighthouse. She played with the edge of the legal pad.

"There will be several tests, both verbal and visual, that I will ask you to take during our sessions together."

"Fine with me," Allie said. But he was beginning to squirm in his seat. It had nothing to do with Dr. Carlotta C. Green. It had to do with another doctor—Dr. D. Q. Nightingale. The conversation early in the morning had stayed with him. Particularly that name: Sarah Lukacs.

He had called her Lewis by mistake. But now the real name, Lukacs, was resonating. He knew that damn name. But how? In what context?

Dr. Green tapped one of the pens on the pad. "You look distraught, Officer Voegler."

"Sorry."

"Let me get some basic information from you, other than what I found in your folder."

"Shoot."

"Have you ever struck a witness in custody before?"

"No."

"Have you ever used physical force during an arrest?"

"No." Allie was thinking of his attack on Lawrence Eisle. But he wasn't about to arrest him. As for the past—well . . . Drag racers. Hopheads. Drunk hunters. Who remembered? Who cared? A few ugly scenes, but for the most part he went by the book. And Hillsbrook wasn't Detroit.

"Why did you want to become a police officer?"

"I couldn't break into the movies. And I couldn't get into med school."

"Why did you join the police force in the town in which you were raised?"

"Is that unusual?"

"Actually, yes. Quite unusual. A neighboring town or county is usually preferred. How long did you know the murdered officer?"

"About two years."

"Were you friends?"

"I don't know how to answer that. But I know where you're heading."

"Where is that, Officer Voegler? Where am I heading?"

"From Chung to Della Hope."

"Right. Simple cause and effect. You lose a friend; you lose control. Is that what happened, Officer Voegler?"

She opened a drawer, pulled out a pack of cigarettes, thought better of it, replaced the pack and closed the drawer. He tried to see what brand she was smoking, but he could not. His vision was blurred. I need glasses, he thought.

"I'm not excusing my actions," he said.

"Good. Don't. It's the oldest scam in the book," she replied, laughing.

The word "scam" sat him bolt upright. Recall! Yes! The goddamn recall. He remembered what Sarah Lukacs was all about. Allie propelled himself out of his chair.

"What is it, Officer Voegler?"

Allie walked out quickly. He retraced his steps down the hallway, down the stairs, and out of the building.

Then he began to run.

Chapter 8

It had been a very long ride down Route 9 in the cab of the concrete-mixer truck. The rains came and went, came and went. Traffic tangled and untangled. The driver kept up a cacophonous account of his and his family's ills, and then turned to political diatribes against the state government and, above all, the New York state troopers who persisted in giving him tickets for operating an unsafe vehicle.

By the time they reached the Holland Tunnel it was noon. And then the driver dropped Charlie on the Jersey side, which presented something of a problem, since no pedestrian traffic was allowed through the tunnel into New York.

Thus Charlie was forced to hitch another ride, this time in a small van owned by a plumbing supply wholesaler. The driver was Dominican and he was well acquainted with the area where Charlie was headed—Hanover Square. In fact, he was going to the Fulton Fish Market, which was right next to the South Street Seaport, which was only four blocks from Hanover Square.

Charlie found himself surrounded by all manner of seafood early that afternoon, the chilly air heavy with the scent of fish entrails. The market was closing, most of its business being conducted in the early morning hours. He was famished, not even able to recall when he'd last eaten. And since even Bodhisattvas got hungry once in a while, he decided he'd better start shaking his alms bowl. He had no doubt that someone would give him something. Some steaming chowder would be most welcomed. But he would have accepted anything, even a raw fish. Even a raw fish head.

He stationed himself in his robe (actually a bathrobe) and sandals (actually rubbers) and held out the bowl of life.

No one threw a fish his way, not even a teeny-weeny sardine. No one took any notice whatever of him. Still he waited. The rain was just a slow drip now. He was getting cold, particularly his toes. After about an hour he made contact with a compassionate soul. The man had walked past him, stopped, shaken his head, then turned and walked back. This kind stranger was short and powerfully built and was chewing on an unlit cigar. He was wearing rain gear much like a fireman's, but he had no hat on and his head was soaking wet.

"Never saw you around here before," the

stranger said, giving Charlie an appraising glance. "See plenty of homeless, but never you."

"I come from upstate," Charlie told him.

"Well, be sure to keep taking your medicine," said the man, and with some effort reached up under his wet slicker, pulled out a stuffed, worn leather wallet, and removed a five-dollar bill, which he placed in Charlie's bowl. Then he walked off, or rather, as Charlie observed, waddled off. The man moved like a drunken sailor.

Charlie scooped up the hill and meandered over to the shopping mall pier in the seaport right next to the moored nineteenth-century clipper ship. He studied the floor plan. On the third floor, it read, was the "Festival of Edibles." Up he went on the escalator, smiling benignly at the security guard who seemed to be fascinated with his ascent.

There certainly was a lot of food on the third floor. He circled the feast of various ethnic goodies. He decided that given his present incarnation and mission it would be best to go with something with an Asian accent. He ordered a plate of pork fried rice and took it to the massive enclosed eating area which thrust out like a cockpit over the East River.

He ate very slowly, enjoying every mouthful. He chewed with precision and thoroughness because he had the feeling, even though it wasn't specified in Lady Barraclough's manual, that there was a right way and a wrong way for a Bodhisattva to take nourishment.

After he was finished he positively cooed at how well his mission was going. He was very close to the prize: Diane Riggins was a mere four blocks away. He wondered if she had any intimation that her Bodhisattva was so close by.

As for the river below, the East River, running to sea, it made Charlie very happy.

He wondered what Mrs. Tunney and the others were doing right then. And Doc Quinn. He knew they were wishing him well; he knew they understood.

He looked up rather than out. The rain drops were splattering on the overhead glass. Each one a life, each one a death, he thought.

Should he go now? He was a bit weary. Perhaps a little rest was called for. Bodhisattvas, he figured, were usually younger men.

He took out Lady Barraclough's classic again. The cover was getting shredded. He dried the book carefully with a paper napkin and then began to read the section on how the Bodhisattva conducts himself in the world, concentrating on those pages that he had not studied carefully before.

One particular sentence caught his eye: "According to the Mahayana tradition, the Earthly Bodhisattvas can, at their own discretion, assume any bodily form and appearance which is appropriate for the help they intend to give.

My, he thought, that is something. He read on.

There are many examples of Bodhisattvas who have assumed different forms in order to quicken the liberation of other beings. They have become aged men, ill men, corpses.

They have become courtesans to attract men. Then, having lured them with the hook of craving, they proceeded to lead the craver to the Buddha-knowledge.

Time and time again they have become poor villagers, caravan leaders, priests, ministers, shoemakers, candle makers, fishermen, and artists, to name just a few.

Charlie closed the book and thought about what he had read. He wondered if he had that power; most certainly he did. Was it necessary at this time to transform himself, prior to his visit to Diane Riggins? He thought and thought and then came to the conclusion that it really wasn't necessary at this time. He would hold those powers in abeyance.

His eyes were beginning to droop. Just a very quick nap, he thought, and I'll go. He lay his face on the cold table next to the empty plate.

Didi and Rose sat on makeshift chairs in the barn. Between them and the stove lay the backpack. The dogs had discovered the object and were playing a canine variety of King of the Hill. Bozo leaped to the top of it and growled, then Huck leaped up and engaged with him in a mock battle, then both ran off and returned in a fury.

"It's like one of those old pirate movies," Rose noted.

Aretha had tired of the game quickly and clambered up on the bag where she parked herself, resting her nose on her paws. Out of deference to her age and sex, Huck and Bozo moved their game elsewhere.

"What are you going to do with it?" Rose asked.

"Bring it to Allie, I suppose."

"You don't sound too enthusiastic about that option."

"Or we can bring it to the Hillsbrook police."

"I suppose so."

It is an ugly backpack, Didi thought. Not streamlined at all.

"What do you think's in it?" asked Rose.

"I don't know."

Rose laughed and asked in a mock serious voice: "And what is our responsibility under the circumstances, Madam Chairwoman?"

"My responsibility, for one, is to my practice. And I haven't even picked up the phone to call home for my messages. I should find out what's happening there."

"These are dark times, girlfriend, and in dark times many things are forgiven."

"Did Thoreau say that?"

"No. I said it."

Didi pulled closer to the stove. Rose was right.

These were indeed dark times—whatever that meant. She looked out the open barn door—dark and wet. "Do you have any wine?" she asked.

"Isn't it a bit early?"

"Obviously not for me."

"In that case, yes I do. I have some good cheap Finger Lakes region white. I put it in dry ice."

"Let me have a glass."

Rose left her chair, retrieved the bottle and poured wine into two cups, rather than glasses. She sat back down.

"How do you like it?" Rose asked.

"It's tolerable," replied Didi. "You want to hear something funny?"

"You know I do. I love a good joke."

Didi used her cup to point to the backpack. "I have a feeling it's all there."

"What's all there?"

"The answers."

"To what?"

"To the murderous everything."

"Poetic," Rose chided her.

"Not only do I think the answers are in there; I have the strange feeling that if we don't find those answers, the times are going to get even darker."

"Go with your intuition, girlfriend."

"If we open that backpack, Rose, we will be doing something very wrong."

"How can it be wrong if the answers are there?"

"Get Aretha off it, will you?"

Rose called the dog's name and Aretha slowly climbed down and sought rest elsewhere.

"Let's finish the wine," Didi said.

"By all means."

They polished off the bottle, placed their cups gently on the ground, walked over to the back-pack, and opened the first clasp.

The first items to surface were shirts, seven of them. Short-sleeved summer sport shirts, all carefully folded. Rose and Didi unfolded each, checked out its pockets, refolded it, and placed it on the ground.

"Why wouldn't he keep these in the motel room?" asked Rose. "Seems kind of dumb, doesn't it? I mean, who would steal them?"

Didi only shrugged. She pulled out the next clump of items, which turned out to be linen and silk handkerchiefs.

"I didn't know men still used things like this," said Rose.

"Maybe they're heirlooms."

Then Didi pulled out a sleeping bag. She opened it, examined it, and refolded it.

Next they found three pairs of jeans, laundered. A formal white shirt of the kind usually worn with a tuxedo. A cummerbund.

"Now it's getting interesting," Didi muttered as she found and pulled out a large, weighty manila envelope.

It had one of those fastening cords, but the string was too knotted to manipulate. Rose brought a scissor and cut it off. "We have now gone beyond the legal," she said conspiratorially. Then she let out a little yelp. "Look, Didi, there's something in the corner." She reached into the backpack once more and extracted several pairs of silk pajamas that had been rolled in the most awkward way imaginable and fastened with a large rubber band. Rose pulled off the band and unrolled one pair.

"Did Wynton wear things like that?" asked Didi.

"Are you kidding? Never. You think I'd go to bed with somebody who wore those things?"

"All right, all right."

Didi opened the envelope and shook out the contents. She went over the items one by one. There were several official-looking papers held with a clip; they seemed to deal with the Hillsbrook Police Department's pension and health benefits program.

There was a passport application, never executed. There were several family photos, including one of a young woman who must have been Chung's deceased mother. There was a packet of money order receipts indicating that sometime before he joined the Hillsbrook police, Wynton had paid back a bank loan.

The bulk of the envelope was comprised of bank statements, dozens and dozens of them, with canceled checks included.

"This isn't what we're looking for," Didi said angrily.

"The problem is, we don't really know what we're looking for."

"I'll know it when I find it," said Didi.

Rose pointed to the nearly empty backpack. "Look there, Didi. The only thing left is his lunch pail. Is a peanut butter sandwich going to help?"

Didi stared at the gaily painted lunch box, the only object left in the bag. It was the kind of pail her mother said she used to carry to school each day.

"He didn't know how to pack a bag properly," Rose noted. "That's why it seemed like there was so much in it."

Didi pulled the lunch pail out and opened the two clips on its front. But then she stopped. She had heard an odd sound. When she looked up, she saw that Rose was crying.

"What's the matter, Rose?"

"It's just . . . I was suddenly thinking of him again. Wynton. I joke around a lot but I'm not a party girl, Didi. He didn't deserve to die. He really was a nice guy."

Didi opened the top of the lunch box. What she saw startled her so much that she drew back. Her movement prompted Rose to peer inside the box.

The box was empty save for three small rectangular white envelopes, each about the size of an invitation to a children's birthday party.

There was something so menacing, so pristine about the unmarked white squares in that antiquated box that Didi felt a rush of excitement. This was it, she felt. Whatever "it" might be.

"Well, go ahead!" Rose urged. "Open the damn things."

Didi picked up the first envelope. It wasn't sealed. Slowly she opened it and removed the piece of newsprint it held.

When the paper was opened up it proved to be yet another photograph. No date appeared, but judging from the clothing of the figures pictured, Didi estimated that the newspaper dated back about ten years. Behind the figures a waiting bus was clearly visible.

The photograph was captioned: MID-HUDSON OPERA GUILD ON ANNUAL TRIP TO METROPOLITAN OPERA.

A squib accompanying the photo read: "Members of the five county association of opera lovers left Thursday for one of their biannual trips to Manhattan. This trip will include a stay at the Hotel Empire and the Metropolitan Opera's new production of *Madama Butterfly*."

"Why on earth would he be saving something like that, Didi?"

"I haven't the slightest idea."

"Do you recognize any of those people?"

"I'm looking."

Carefully, face by face, Didi perused the somewhat blurred photo. "There!" she cried.

"What? What is it?"

"This face. Look. Do you know who that is?"

"No."

"Walter Stringfellow."

"Really? Are you sure?"

"Yes."

"What about the others?"

"Not anyone I know."

She reached into the box and pulled out the next envelope. Inside it was a single index card. And on that card were five telephone numbers written in large, bold numerals.

Didi studied the numbers. None were familiar. She passed the card to Rose. "Take a look."

"No. I don't know any of those numbers. The top three have no area code, so they must be Dutchess County. The bottom two have 718 and 516 codes. That's either Brooklyn, Queens, or the Bronx, and Long Island."

Didi took the index card back, laid it on the envelope which had contained it, and slowly removed the third and last envelope. That she opened, and shook the contents out onto the barn floor.

"Polaroid shots," said Rose.

"Indeed they are," Didi said, and lined them up for easy viewing.

Each snapshot showed a mare and a foal in a somewhat less than lush grazing area.

"Horses. *Horses?* Weird," Rose said. "More weirdness. He never talked about horses to me."

Didi felt her excitement growing. It was like examining a sick cow, noting the symptoms, and then letting the symptom cluster metamorphose into a rational diagnosis. Oh, there was no diagnosis here, but there sure was one whopping symptom.

She plucked one of the photos up. "Look at this," she told Rose, who dutifully looked. "Remember when I told you I had visited Lorenz's place to treat a filly?"

"Yes, I remember."

"That's the bay filly, here in this photo, and that's her mother."

"What about the horses in the other pictures?"

"I don't know. But I do know this pair. I'm sure of it."

"Okay, so you're sure. So what?"

Didi didn't answer the question. She picked up the index card with the numbers and handed it to Rose. "Do me a favor, Rose. Start calling these phone numbers now."

"What should I say?"

"Just find out who they belong to."

Rose took the card, found her cellular phone, and positioned herself almost outside the barn door, where the telephone reception and transmission were always clearer.

Didi waited, rocking back and forth a bit, staring at the photo with the bay pair, moving and shifting the unfamiliar photos, as if by changing their positions she would learn something.

She could hear Rose making the calls but she

couldn't make out the conversations. The whole task took only five minutes.

"Two of them had machines," Rose reported. "I got through to three."

"And?"

"They're truckers. Horse truckers."

"You mean vanners."

"Yeah, I guess so. They transport horses."

Didi's face became anguished. "What's the matter?" Rose asked. "Did I do something wrong?"

Didi picked up her wine cup and began to pace. She walked three times around the stove. Then she picked up the photos and sat down heavily. "Listen, Rose."

"I'm listening."

"We are dealing with horses and murder, right?"

"If you say so."

"Well, it's out in the open. Chung took photos of horses and he was murdered. That piano player was carrying miniature fake horse documents and she was murdered. Robert Lorenz for some reason or another kept horses as well as dairy cows and he was blown away."

"I guess you have a point."

"Now answer me this. What was the relationship between that piano player and Chung?"

"None that we know of. Right? Except that she played the tunes at that restaurant on the night he died."

"Right. The relationship is fuzzy. We don't know. Maybe she made a call to someone saying that Chung was there and that someone got his weapon and blew him away. Whatever . . . it is fuzzy. But the relationship between Robert Lorenz and Chung was not fuzzy at all. Was it?"

"No. Not really. He made those monthly payments to Chung."

"Exactly. Eighty-eight dollars a month. And Mr. Lorenz gave us a fake explanation for the payments."

"That's what we think."

"Now tell me, Rose. There were two other people who had that exact same relationship to Chung. Weren't there?"

"Yes. That other dairy farmer, Prosper. And Cynthia Bracken."

"Right. Eighty-eight bucks and a fake cover story."

Didi picked up the two photos that were unidentified. She flashed them at Rose. "You see?"

"The only thing I see is . . . horses."

"These horses were photographed on Prosper's land and the Brackens' land. They own these horses."

"Did you see horses on Prosper's land?"

"No," Didi admitted. "Nor did I see any at the Bracken sisters' place. But Lorenz had them well hidden from view, far back on his property. The others probably did the same."

"Okay. Even if they have those horses, so what? What does that mean?"

"It means they're going to die next."

"Do you know what you're saying, Didi?"

"Yes. Whoever this madman is, he is rolling something up. Boom. Boom. Boom. And the logic next leads to either Cynthia Bracken or Prosper—and I think both."

"Then you'd better call the Hillsbrook police."

"That Chief Gough would laugh at us."

"Then call Allie."

"What can he do? He's been told to stay out of the Hillsbrook area for the time being if he wants his job back."

"So what are you suggesting? I get the feeling that you are about to suggest something. Or course you can call those people and warn them."

"I'm sure they already have an inkling of what's in store for them. I think we have to concentrate on one thing: the murderer. To either stop him or identify him."

"And how do we do that?"

"Very simple. We watch Prosper and Bracken. We leave the red Jeep here because it'll be recognized. We take your car. I drive you to Prosper and set you up in one of the clumps of trees that abut his property. Just put on some rain gear, take Aretha and your cellular phone. I then drive to the Bracken place and, as they say in the detective novels, stake it out. The minute anyone shows, the minute anyone sets foot on their property, make the call and get a license plate or description."

Rose took a long time to digest the plan. At last, she said, "Didi, this is a very dangerous undertaking. We're not talking about a Peeping Tom here. This person has already killed two people. At least two, and possibly a third."

"I am aware of that."

"How brave should we be? I want to be a nature girl, not a commando."

"As brave as you feel."

"And you're talking about tonight?"

"No. I'm talking about now. Chung was murdered at night. But the other two in broad daylight. Now, Rose. We go there now or we don't go at all."

"Do you really feel this is the right thing?"

"In my veterinary work, Rose, I'm right about fifty percent of the time. That's about all I can promise you."

Rose leaned over and scratched Aretha's ear. Then she looked up. "Which rain hat? The red? Or maybe the black. It's more funereal."

They drove a full twenty miles east on Route 28 before either of them said a word.

It was the driver, Art Moldava, who spoke, and he wasn't happy.

"Do me a favor, Allie. Don't ever do that again."

"Do what?"

"Barge into where I work and drag me out on some kind of fake emergency."

"It's not fake."

"Then what's it about? Why do I have to drive you to Hillsbrook? Why don't you go yourself? You have a car."

"I may need your help."

"You damn well may. You're not supposed to set foot in the Hillsbrook area."

"I know that."

"I had to cancel practice."

"Which one? Hell, Art, they pay you peanuts and you coach football, soccer, and wrestling at that private school."

"This is Otsego County, my friend. I'm lucky to have any job at all. And it's the football practice I'm talking about."

"What's the team's record?"

"So far, three losses."

"No wins?"

"No."

"So what the hell is one practice more or less?"

"It can mean plenty."

"Okay. Believe me, I wouldn't have pulled you away if it wasn't important. I'll buy you dinner when we get back."

Art grumbled but said nothing else for another ten minutes. Allie kept opening and closing the window. Sometimes he lit a cigarette only to snub it out quickly.

"You are looking for trouble, aren't you? I mean, when a police chief tells one of his detectives to stay the hell out of Hillsbrook and said detective just drives on in . . . well, you do know you're asking for trouble?"

"Trouble is a relative term."

Art Moldava found that hugely funny. After the

chuckles had died out: "I suppose when they get rid of you I can get you a job as assistant soccer coach."

"I don't know anything about soccer."

"So what? Do you think I do?"

Allie didn't answer. He shifted his weight in the seat and for the first time Art saw the sidearm.

"What are you doing carrying that?"

"Carrying what?"

"The weapon."

"I'm a cop. I carry a weapon."

"Not from what you told me. You told me the weapon was taken away from you for the time being. Until the hearing."

"Just drive, Art."

Silence for another ten miles.

"Do you have any gum?" Art asked.

"No."

"Good. I hate gum. Now tell me about this girl-friend of yours or ex girlfriend, or fiancée, or whatever she is."

"Some other time, Art."

"To be honest, I spoke to her once and I don't like her."

"Why?"

"It's not what she said. It was how she said it."

"She is kind of rough on the phone."

"Rough? She sounds like a drill sergeant."

"You're exaggerating, Art. She does have a kind of . . . well . . . I guess you can call it an interrogatory style. But she's a vet. She's dealing with a whole bunch of psychotic dairy farmers. They can't see straight much less talk straight. So she has to cut through the crap."

As they approached Kingston Allie became more and more tense. Art could feel it. Tense and maybe a little bit unstable. He began playing with an unlit cigarette. "You look like you're going to the shootout at the O.K. Corral," Art noted.

Allie kept staring straight ahead. Art was no longer angry at his friend for this imposition, but he was getting a little apprehensive. An out-of-control Allie Voegler with a weapon he shouldn't have, about to enter an area he had been ordered to stay out of. Well, that was a bit chancy.

"Maybe we should stop for a bite," he suggested.

"Keep driving, Art."

"Okay, Sarge. May I stop for gas when the tank is empty?"

"Don't call me Sarge."

"What does she call you?"

"Who?"

"The vet."

"She calls me Allie."

"My ex-wife always called me Arthur. Tell me, is she good in bed?"

"I never slept with your ex-wife."

"Very funny. I meant the Nightingale."

"I don't know."

"You mean you never slept with her?"

"Of course I have. I mean, who gives a damn if

someone you love is good in bed? She can come into the bedroom dressed like the Virgin Mary or Joan of Arc or Mae West or a sadomasochistic transvestite or Lady Dracula. She could lay on the bed like a bag of potatoes or she can lead me through the entire Kama Sutra. It don't matter. You get it, Art? I love her."

"Take it easy, Allie. Just take it easy. You're over-reacting."

Silence reigned again, an awkward silence, until they crossed the Hudson and entered Dutchess County. Then Allie said, "Pull over, Art."

"Now?"

"Yes."

"For what? Let's wait until we hit a diner."

"No. Now."

Art slowed down and pulled the car off the road onto the shoulder.

"Turn the ignition off," Allie said. Art did so. "I just want to say a few things to you," Allie said.

"I'm listening."

"I'm sorry about barging in like that. I'm sorry about all this mystery. But I need you, Art. I need a wheel man."

Art laughed. "What are we going to do? Rob a bank?"

"No. But we may have to move fast and I'm not in the best of shape, Art."

"I know that."

"So I need someone with me I can depend on.

Someone to drive. Someone to keep me on the straight and narrow."

"Okay, Allie. I get the picture. I'm with you."

"A few hours ago I was sitting in a shrink's office. And I remembered something. Something very important about a lady called Sarah Lukacs who lives in Clinton Corners."

"Is that where we're going?"

"No. We're going to a place on the outskirts of Hillsbrook. But listen to me. It's important. You know what has been going on in Hillsbrook, don't you?"

"I heard on the radio."

"A whole lot of ugly killing, Art. And what I remembered about this lady might stop it. Might end it. I'm not sure but I have a gut feeling that it will. So it doesn't really matter to me that I'm carrying a weapon that I shouldn't be carrying. Do you understand? And it doesn't matter to me that I might lose my job if I enter the town limits of Hillsbrook. Get it? Am I making myself clear?"

"Loud and clear. Just tell me when to jump and I'll jump, Allie."

"Are you sure? I need you, Art. But I need you with no holds barred. I appreciate your putting me up. I know I've been a pain in the ass. But what I'm talking about now is three people shot to death. And maybe more to come."

Art rolled up the sleeve on his right arm and thrust the tattoo that he had gotten many years ago outside Camp Lejeune, North Carolina, a few weeks after they had finished boot camp. It read "Semper Fi."

Allie nodded. Art started the vehicle and they drove on.

A half hour later, under Allie's instructions, Art guided the car up a bumpy overgrown path and stopped in front of a ramshackle, decaying Winnebago motor home set on cinder blocks.

"I ain't seen a squat this ugly since I left North Carolina," Art said.

Then he cocked his head. "Listen, Allie . . . hear it? Now that ain't ugly at all."

Both men in the car listened to the strains of an operatic aria drifting out from the Winnebago.

"I think that's Maria Callas," Allie said. " 'Un Bel Di,' from *Madama Butterfly*."

A dog had him by the arm and was pulling and growling. Charlie groaned and woke up. He didn't know where he was. A strange man in a strange outfit was shaking him awake. "You've been here for hours, man. You're going to have to vacate the premises now."

Charlie sat back. My goodness, he must have just conked out right after he ate the pork fried rice. The empty dish was still next to him.

"Who are you, brother?" Charlie asked gently.

"Security."

"Could I bother you for the time?"

"About five-thirty. Are you going to go quiet, or what?"

The man was being distinctly unfriendly. Quiet? Of course he would be quiet. Why wouldn't he be quiet?

Charlie shrugged and got to his feet. He'd been asleep for four hours. It was time to get to Hanover Square. He smoothed his robe, made sure he had his cane and bowl, and set out for the escalator.

The rainy streets were choked with people leaving work and heading down into the subways. Charlie picked his way through the crowds, searching for the correct address. Ah, there was Hanover Square!

He stopped in front of the most imposing edifice on the square, a massive, polished stone building which, according to the plaque near the doorway, had once held the Cotton Exchange and had been converted to cooperative apartments in 1985.

He strode through the heavy glass doors to a desk in the center of the lobby, where a uniformed doorman was writing in a ledger.

"Miss Diane Riggins," Charlie announced clearly. "I'm here to see her."

Never looking up from his chores, the doorman said, "You're going to miss the champagne. The party started an hour and a half ago. Apartment 5C."

Charlie did not know what the man was talking about, but he thanked him anyway and headed toward the elevator.

Just then, the doorman looked up and let out a

bellow of rage. He raced past Charlie and blocked his route to the elevator.

"What the hell do you think you're doing, fella? Get out of here before I call the cops."

Charlie smiled.

The doorman seized him by the arm. "I told you bums before: no soliciting in the lobby. Now get your raggedy ass out of here."

Charlie braced his legs and brought his cane down sharply on the man's knees. The doorman cried out. Charlie was suffused with sudden shame at his total abandonment under pressure of the Bodhisattva vow. He knew immediately what a terrible thing he had just done.

"I'm sorry!" he cried, grief-stricken. "Let me help you to a chair, brother. It's just that . . . well, I don't think you understand. I'm a friend of Miss Riggins. From Hillsbrook."

A shadow of fear creased the doorman's face. He might have made a job-threatening mistake.

"You mean you were at that retreat with Miss Riggins?"

"It's a wonderful thing, that retreat," Charlie said—not exactly an answer.

A look of contrition came over the doorman's face. He launched into an apology, but Charlie stopped him: "No harm done, brother. Looks like my robes might be worrisome to a lot of city people."

Charlie patted the man lightly on the back and walked into the waiting elevator. The fifth-floor hallway was vaulted and lined with plush carpeting. It was like walking in a deep alfalfa pasture. He was in front of number 5C now.

Something was odd. The door was half open and from within came the sounds of many voices and music. Charlie pushed the door open and stepped inside.

What had the fellow downstairs said about champagne? Charlie understood it now. There was a cocktail party in progress. Men in those soft-looking high-priced suits from Italy and shirts that cost what some folks paid every month for rent. Funny thing was, some of the women seemed to be wearing identical outfits, except you could see a hell of a lot more of their chests.

Charlie was startled to find a porcine bald man only two or three inches away from his face, staring intently at him. Taking a couple of steps backward, Charlie nodded his greeting at the man.

"What do you mean?" the man asked at last. "What are you trying to *say?*"

"Mean?" said Charlie. "I didn't say anything."

"No, no. I meant your . . . your appearance. What is it that you're trying to say with those . . . ah . . . clothes?"

Another man, much younger, champagne glass in hand, appeared just then. He too was staring at Charlie in puzzlement. "Don't tell me," he said, deadpan. "The pizza's here."

Charlie heard laughter all around him. A crowd had gathered.

Then he saw her—the hostess—the woman—the beautiful Diane. And indeed she was as lovely as ever. So lovely that it made him forget all the people who stood gawking and snickering at him.

Diane was wearing a short black dress cut low in front with thin shoulder straps. A simple pearl necklace completed her outfit.

"Well, Diane," the young man said between sips from his flute, "looks like you've forgotten to make your annual donation to the Hare Krishna Relief Fund. I think you'd better pay up. This guy looks dangerous."

Diane Riggins broke through the knot of revelers and slowly approached Charlie. She was taking unsure, tentative steps, a trace of fear in her stiff smile.

"Are you sure you have the right apartment?" she asked, not unkindly.

"Don't you know me?" Charlie asked, his eyes dancing with pleasure. "It's me—Charlie Gravis. From Hillsbrook."

"Oh my God! Of course. You're the old man who kept following me. Charlie—was that your name?—what are you doing here?"

This was the moment he had planned for, waited for. The moment of declaration.

He would use Master Gotama's words. What else?

"Therefore, Diane," Charlie intoned, "be an island unto yourself, a refuge unto yourself; take the teaching as island, the teaching as refuge. Have no other refuge.'"

The room was utterly silent for a long moment, and then Diane asked, "What?"

Charlie walked close to her. "I am the Bodhisattva you seek."

Diane Riggins burst into merry laughter. The rest of the crowd followed suit. Then she took Charlie by the arm and whispered into his ear: "Listen to me, Charlie. I go to Buddhist retreats just like I go to the health spa. Understand, Charlie—you sweet, crazy old thing?"

"Here, Diane." It was the bald man, holding out a champagne bottle to his hostess. "Give this to Maharishi Mambo. Maybe he'll bless us with some insider information on commodity prices."

A lowing sound rolled toward them from the back of the room then. It grew louder and louder as it rolled. Some of the guests were spoofing the meditational "Ommmm."

The merriment went out of control then. Charlie wasn't sure how it happened—did someone trip, or was it done purposefully—but he ended up drenched in Bollinger champagne.

The hours had dripped away like the rain, slowly, steadily. It was now dark and foggy and the Bracken sisters seemed to have hunkered down for the evening.

Didi sat in the battered old Volvo across and up the road from the Bracken house. From time to time she switched positions, moving from the driver seat to the passenger seat. But nothing seemed to allow enough room for her legs. She had a clear view of the two-lane road, a clear view of the house, and a clear view of its frontage. On the dashboard were her cellular phone, a pair of binoculars, and a flashlight. All sensible items to have brought along on a mission like this one.

However, as the hours passed and she sat fantasizing about a cup of steaming hot coffee, she realized more and more acutely how poorly she had prepared for the stakeouts—both her own and Rose's. She had grabbed a handful of unsalted cashews from the cupboard at Rose's place, but had long ago consumed them. And why had she not thought to bring blankets? The car engine had to remain off and the lights out, so there was no using the heater.

And then the guilt over what poor Rose must be enduring began to eat at her. Didi was ashamed of herself for summarily deciding that it would be she, not Rose, who waited in the car. However chilly she felt sitting inside the Volvo, Rose must have been twice as bad off out there in the elements.

Her reasoning for the decision—a belief that one of the Bracken sisters would be the next target for murder—was based on a kind of geographical logic: the last murder had been in the center of Hillsbrook and the Brackens were closer to the center of town than Willy Prosper. Thus it should be Didi who acted as sentry for the sisters and took on the greater risk. But the more she thought about it, the more she doubted her thinking; it might just as well have been self-serving. In other words, maybe she simply wanted the protection of the Volvo for herself.

Well, at least Rose had Aretha out there. The big old shepherd bitch would be both company and security.

She leaned back against the car seat and tried to relax her entire body. This was just one, ongoing nightmare, wasn't it? From the moment she and Wynton had waltzed out onto that parking lot, up to the present torment, stuck here in Rose's old wreck of a car—one horrible event after another.

It was no good. She couldn't relax. God, if only she had something to do, something to keep her hands occupied. And something that required no light. Didi thought enviously, crazily, of all the possessed women she'd seen over a lifetime who could sit knitting for hours without even glancing down.

And what about people, like her mother, who played solitaire for hours on end? There was one variation—diamond solitaire, it was called—her mother was a whiz at it and she had dozens of times tried unsuccessfully to teach her daughter how to play. You build a diamond of cards with five rows and then remove the cards from the diamond by having two cards equal the numerical equivalent of thirteen—well, who besides her mom could keep track of it?

She grimaced in the darkness. Why did all thoughts of late seem ultimately to lead back to her late mother's life and death? Did it have something to do with the difficulties with Allie?

She realized she rarely thought now of her mother during good times . . . only during the bad times. She loved her even more in the bad times, but the memories ought to be balanced. After all, the woman herself had been all about balance. Complex, yes; indefatigable, yes; stronger than Didi, and wilder, but balanced. She ran a home and a family and she helped anyone and everyone she ever met who was in need.

Well, Didi thought, people don't like me the way they liked her. But no cows ever loved my mother like they love me. It was a stupid train of thought and to break it she moved back to the driver's seat, gripped the wheel, and tried to look out into the dark terrain for signs of movement. Nothing. Nothing anyway.

She picked up the binoculars, focused on the house lights. The Bracken sisters were inside, still up. One was reading. The other seemed to be pacing with a cup in her hand. Yes, the one moving about was Cynthia, the presumed target of the murderer.

Didi put the binoculars down all at once. Unbidden, she had had a sudden image of Drew Pelletier. For godsake, why would that face appear to her now? He was her first and only lover. The professor at the University of Pennsylvania School of Veterinary Medicine who had seduced her and then abruptly ended their short but passionate affair. Years later she had encountered him again. Only this time he was the subject of her inquiries into a very nasty, underhanded scheme to make big money at the racetrack. She wondered where he was now. Perhaps in prison, perhaps practicing veterinary medicine in Canada or Europe. Working as a pharmaceutical salesman under an assumed name? Anything was possible—he was an amazingly charming, resourceful, and, unfortunately, devious man.

The affair with Pelletier had been nothing like the one with Allie. Where the former was wild, bold, and unpredictable, the latter was staid. The former was all encompassing, consuming, while the latter was, frankly, mundane. She had loved Drew Pelletier with a kind of runaway ecstasy; with Allie it was almost sisterly.

Dr. Nightingale had relaxed enough to smile. She wondered what other obsessional memories would return if she was forced to spend all night in this car.

She sat up straight, leaned forward a little, and looked at her face in the rearview mirror. Isn't it strange, she thought, that whenever I think of Drew I check out how I look?

Her own face was not the only image she saw in

the mirror. There was another car parked behind hers.

Another car! Not twenty feet away.

She had not seen it arrive. She had not heard it. All its lights were out.

Didi froze in fear.

Her eyes landed on the phone on the dashboard. Make the call! she willed her hand. Pick it up—now! Wait a minute—call who? Where?

Or should she just run? But she was too frightened to get out.

The back window suddenly exploded, glass showering over her head.

Then another window. And another.

She fell upon the passenger door and rolled out of the Volvo. The minute she felt the earth under her feet she scratched, rolled, and fought her way through the mud. She rolled down the incline between the road and the woods. Pain stabbed at her ankle. She tried to stand but could only crouch.

Then she looked up. A figure was standing at the top of the incline, looking down at her. His hands were thrust out, aiming his weapon.

No way out. She could only stare back at him. Her eyes itched from mud and rain. I'm going to die now, Didi was screaming inside her head. I'm dying.

But he did not pull the trigger. He continued to stand there, looking, pointing the gun.

"Shoot! Shoot!" she heard herself scream.

Then two penetrating lights were blinding her.

She turned away, shielding her eyes. Up on level ground, an engine roared. Then the squeal of brakes. And an anguished cry: "Didi! Didi!"

Someone was beside her now. A man. He caught her under the arms and pulled her back up the slope. He was saying something—not just saying something, he was cursing her vehemently.

"Stupid, stupid woman! You idiot!" Again and again he reviled her as he carried her up the incline. Her ankle was white hot with pain now, but she didn't care about that. Not anymore. She knew who it was dragging her back to the road: Allie Voegler.

Allie picked her up and carried her to the spot where his vehicle had crushed the would-be shooter against Rose's. The man had fallen under the Volvo's wheel. He was alive but moaning.

Allie lay her down in the space between the two cars, almost nose to nose with the crumpled assassin.

"Take a look, Dr. Nightingale, take a look!" Allie said. He picked the suffering man's head up from the ground, Herod offering the head of John the Baptist to Salome.

Didi obeyed.

"Does he look familiar? You know him?" Allie shouted.

She could only shake her head no.

"It's Darryl Chung. Wynton's brother." He allowed the head to thud back to the ground. There was blood on Darryl Chung's face. He was attempting to say something, but there was too much blood in his mouth.

Allie sank to the ground beside Didi and buried his face in his hands. She wanted to console him. But she could not. She could not do anything.

He had entered apartment 5C a Bodhisattva. But he left a sopping wet old fool who knew exactly what he was.

The doorman took pity on him and escorted Charlie into the laundry room, which had been closed for the evening by then, gave him a mover's pad to cover his stained old robe, and handed him a fistful of quarters for the pay phone.

There among the spanking white washers and dryers, Charlie fed coins into the slot and called Ike Badian's home phone.

"Charlie? Good God, man, they're looking for you all over tarnation. We've been worried sick. Where the hell are you, anyway?"

"I'm down here in New York City, Ike . . . I'm okay."

"You're where?"

"New York City, I said. Wall Street."

"Charlie, what the—"

"Never mind that now. It's a long story. Look here, I don't have any money. And I'm not feeling so hot."

"I'll come down there and get you."

"I'd appreciate it. It's a long drive, I know. But—"

"No problem, Charlie. I'll take the Taconic to

Saw Mill, and then the West Side Highway, if I'm remembering right."

"Don't think there is a West Side Highway anymore down here."

"What do you mean? What happened to it? I was just on it—in 1972."

Charlie gave Ike the Hanover Square address and directed him as best he could.

"Okay. You just wait there till I come for you. And don't do anything stupid."

Charlie hung up, pulled the quilted rug around him tightly, and climbed up on one of the hard folding tables. If nothing else, it was warm and dry in the room, and if he didn't get some decent shut-eye soon, he knew he'd go crazy. Lord, this was worse than a foxhole on Iwo Jima. He closed his eyes, but just before he fell asleep he had an inspired idea: he pulled out of the wet bathrobe and threw it in one of the machines, shoving a couple of quarters into the slot. Then he lay down again and slept like the dead.

It was almost midnight when Ike arrived in his ancient but serviceable Ford pickup. He was carrying a small bundle under one arm. The doorman led him to the laundry room and left him with his friend, who was slumbering peacefully, his rubber Buddhist slippers beneath his head as a pillow.

"Rise and shine," Ike said, throwing the bundle Charlie's way. "They might not fit, but anything's better than what you're wearing now."

"That's okay. My robe's clean now. A couple of minutes in the dryer and it ought to be—"

"Just put 'em on, Gravis."

Charlie dressed in the old clothes and walked slowly with Ike to the car.

"I had almost no trouble getting down here except I got lost when I was only two blocks away. Take a peek in the glove compartment, Charlie."

The handle to the compartment was fastened with rope, the lock having rusted away long ago. With some difficulty, Charlie undid the rope. He was still dazed and confused a bit. But he was sharp enough to spot the small bottle of Wild Turkey.

"Take yourself a swallow," Ike directed.

Charlie uncapped the bottle and took a swig. The whisky ran through him with white heat. He shook his head like a swimmer with water in his ears.

Charlie then offered the bottle to Ike, who refused it steadfastly. "I'm driving, Charlie."

Charlie closed his eyes, holding the bottle against his chest. "Can I stay at your place, Ike?"

"Sure. But why? They're all waiting to see you."

"I'm embarrassed."

"Ain't no reason to be embarrassed, Charlie. The way I see it, you been on a three-day drunk."

"I wasn't."

"At our age, you can get a three-day drunk over a woman. And that's what happened. Isn't that what happened?"

"Something like that."

"It happens all the time. Like that joke about the old dairy farmer who loses his place and then decides to become a pig farmer. You know that one, Charlie?"

"No."

"Sure you do. You must."

"I don't know the joke, Ike."

"Well, it goes like this . . . Wait a minute, Charlie. Give me a cigar from out of the glove compartment first . . . Thanks." Ike fiddled with the fat cigar for a minute before stuffing it between his teeth. He never got around to lighting it.

"Anyway," he resumed, "it goes like this. Of course the old geezer doesn't have a dime left, but he goes to the bank for a loan. Now, the banker is one of those city characters who's been transferred to the local branch for a little seasoning. He knows pig farming is hot. He knows pig farmers make a lot of money, at least as the market was then. So he gives the old dairy farmer a loan and our boy is back in business. He rents a spread, he buys a herd, he contracts for feed deliveries, he starts pig farming. But about two months after the operation starts he goes back to the bank and asks for another couple of thousand dollars. The banker says to him, 'You couldn't have gone through the whole loan yet.' The old dairy farmer, now successful pig farmer, replies, 'I didn't. I just need some quick cash to buy the milk cans.'"

Ike laughed so hard at the punch line that he almost drove his pickup off the East River Drive.

All Charlie did was drink more whisky. By the time they reached the Saw Mill Parkway the Wild Turkey had sent him into a kind of loquacious, introspective mood. "I know I went around the bend," he said.

"No doubt about that."

"And I know it was about a woman."

"No doubt about that."

"But believe me, Ike, there were a whole lot of other things going on."

"No doubt about that."

"I mean about suffering and craving."

"You're losing me."

"I mean life *is* suffering and the way to end suffering *is* to end craving."

"If you say so."

"What I'm saying is that yes I went around the bend and sure it was about that beautiful lady, that Diane Riggins, and yes I turned into a ridiculous old idiot—but it all made sense at the time and a lot of it makes sense to me now ... right now, Ike ... right now."

"Don't drink too much."

"I'm not a holy roller, Ike."

"You sure ain't."

"But a lot of the stuff I read in that book of your sister's—it made me think in a different way. I stopped thinking about me, about Charlie Gravis.

Because when I looked in the mirror I saw nothing. Do you know what I mean?"

"Nope."

"I was taking a walk, Ike. And I saw this squashed woodchuck. And a hawk was pulling him off the road and a couple of crows wanted some of the woodchuck and there was this kind of battle and that's when . . . well, I guess, Ike . . . if you want to put it like Mrs. Tunney would put it . . . I saw the face of God. A vision."

"I don't want to hear that stuff, Charlie. I really don't go for that stuff. What were you, a Hindu?"

"No, a Buddhist."

"Sure. Six of one. Listen to me, Charlie. If the Lutherans are right, then the Catholics burn in hell. If the Methodists are right, then the Muslims are in trouble. If the Muslims are right, then who knows who is in trouble and it goes on and on and it has been going on for ten thousand years. And I really don't want to talk about this stuff. If I want deep, heavy talk I lean over the stall and talk to Sophie."

"She's a cow, Ike. And she don't write."

"Hell you say. The Hindus think cows are gods, and they leave plenty of messages in the pasture."

"What I'm trying to say, Ike, is that I don't know which part was crazy and which part was smart."

"Let me tell you something, buddy. There you were standing in the middle of Hillsbrook looking like an idiot wearing a pair of rain rubbers and begging for coins with a stupid soup bowl. Believe me, it was all crazy."

Charlie didn't reply. He was fast asleep and he didn't wake until Ike pulled the pickup onto his farm.

Ike helped his friend down from the seat and toward the house. About twenty feet from the door, Ike stopped and said, "Do you want to get cheered up before you sack out, Charlie?"

"Sure."

"I want to show you my new cow. You didn't know I had new head of stock, did you?"

"When did that happen?"

"Just the other day. Oh, he's a beauty. He's in the cow barn now."

"He? A bull? What's he doing in the cow barn? You're asking for trouble, Ike."

"Naw, this one is no trouble. Take a peek."

He led Charlie into the cow barn and toward the rear. "He's in the last stall on the left. Go ahead, look." He released Charlie's arm, who walked over to the stall and peered in.

Charlie literally jumped back after he looked in. "Are you crazy, Ike? There's a horse in there."

Ike bubbled over with laughter. He was enjoying himself immensely. He walked quickly over to Charlie and regrabbed his arm. "Is that the funniest scene you've ever seen?" he crowed. The two old dairymen stared at the dappled colt, lying on its side and snoring lightly.

"You won't believe what happened, Charlie."

"Probably not."

"The other day I go out to bring the herd in and I see this clown here grazing along with my cows, not a worry in the world. So I say to myself, after I make sure I haven't gone around the bend like you, he probably just run off from somewhere and I'll get the cows in and then he'll run back where he came from. But no. He follows the cows into the barn, parks himself in a stall, finds the feed to his liking, and just settles in."

"What are you going to do with him?"

"I don't know. Got any suggestions?"

Charlie shook his head slowly. They headed back toward the house. Suddenly Charlie panicked, reaching into his pockets wildly.

"What's the matter?"

"Lady Barraclough. I lost her. I can't find Lady Barraclough."

"Another one of your lady friends?"

"No. She's the one who wrote that book I found in your sister's library."

"Well, Charlie, don't worry about it. You saw how many other books there are up there. Help yourself in the morning. Why don't you try one of them on the Dervishes? I kind of liked it when she tried to spin around like them, chanting and everything. She fell smack down on her back and had to be in bed for two weeks."

"Sure, maybe the Dervishes," Charlie muttered. They walked into the house.

* * *

The inside of Rose's barn was illuminated by battery-operated flashlights set along the walls of the barn and hanging from various rafters. Since she had no electricity, she had opted for battery power rather than kerosene lanterns, which were dangerous. The scene looked like the setting for a Romanian gypsy drama.

Next to the stove sat Dr. Deirdre Quinn Nightingale. Her lower left leg was heavily bandaged. She had been sent to the same emergency ward that had admitted Darryl Chung. Only she had been released in an hour with the diagnosis of torn ligaments and no breaks.

Behind Didi stood Rose, who was carefully and slowly picking slivers of glass from Didi's denim jacket.

About ten feet away, lying on one of Rose's ubiquitous mats, lay Art Moldava, playing with all three of the dogs.

They were all waiting for Allie Voegler. After the state troopers and the Hillsbrook cops had cleaned up the crime scene and the wounded had been dispatched to hospitals and the wrecked cars to the police lot, Allie had gone with Chief Gough back to police headquarters.

He had been there for three hours at least. He had to be at the barn shortly. Rose had tried to pump Art Moldava for information as to how events had unfolded, and why, but Allie's friend had refused to answer her questions.

So there was just silence and the lights from the

battery ashtrays and once in a while a bark from one of the dogs playing with Art. Even Aretha, who usually did not frolic, seemed to like the stranger from Cooperstown. Rose did not. She didn't like Moldava one bit. As for Didi, she had other things on her mind, including the throbbing in her ankle.

Allie arrived at one-forty-five, to find everyone in attendance—Art, Rose, Didi, the dogs—in a complete stupor.

But the moment he entered the barn the atmosphere changed. It became electric with his anger.

He strode over to Didi, stopped about five feet away from her, pointed a finger, and shouted: "You are a very stupid woman." He then pointed at Rose. "And you are not much smarter."

Then he turned, walked five steps back, turned, and approached her again. He was getting angrier and angrier.

"You shouldn't be alive now. Do you understand that? Do you hear what I am saying? What you did was so crazy and so dangerous as to be beyond belief. You want to kill yourself, Didi? Just tell me. I'll give you a gun. You can shoot yourself. Why go through all that bother like you did?"

He walked away and came back again, arms flailing. "I hope you are listening to me, Dr. Nightingale. I hope you know that it was only the slightest of flukes that saved your life. I hope you realize that the only reason you are sitting here now and not in the morgue is because of a fluke.

Because there were two ways to get from point A to point B and I decided on x rather than y. That's why you're still among the living. A thousand to one. No, a million to one. If I was a betting man those are the odds I'd give against you coming out of that thing alive." He turned to his friend. "Am I telling the truth, Art?"

"You sure are."

Didi finally spoke. "Is the performance finished? Can you tell me what you're talking about?"

Her question seemed to deflate Allie totally. He literally crumbled with exhaustion and sat down with his back against the barn wall. He lit a cigarette.

"You can't smoke in my barn," Rose said.

Allie ignored her. He spoke to Didi. "Okay, okay, I'm going to take it from the top."

"Please do."

"Remember that lady you mentioned to me the other day on the phone?"

"You mean Sarah Lukacs? The one Wynton was supplying with goat cheese?"

"Yeah. A few hours after that call I'm sitting in the shrink's office and I remember her. She was one of the widows who was scammed by a man named Sherman Porter. This was one of Wynton's first legitimate cases. And he got the victims to talk by befriending them. Sherman Porter just got out of jail. In fact I talked to him briefly after Wynton was shot. But he couldn't tell me anything. Anyway, after I remember who Sarah Lukacs is, I remember you saying that Chung also supplied alkies with booze from those monthly payments he got. And I remembered that Porter had an awful lot of brandy lying around. So I realize that Wynton kept in touch with both Porter and Lukacs. That old drunk was lying to me, I realized. But why and about what? So me and Art drove down to sweat him."

Allie stubbed the cigarette out with his fingers. "Can I have a beer, Rose?"

"No."

Allie gave her a dirty look but continued. "We get to Porter's place. We sweat him. He won't say a goddamn word. I decide the best thing is to take him to the Hillsbrook P.D. and let them sweat him. I'm not even supposed to be in the county."

Allie got up laboriously and began to pace before he spoke.

"Porter doesn't want to come along. He puts up a fight. I cuff him and throw him in Art's car. We head toward the center of town. Now you know, Didi, there are two ways to town from the Ridge. I take the long one—don't ask me why—the one that goes past Rose's place—this place.

"It's dark already but I'll be damned if I don't see your Jeep parked there. So I pull over to say hello. But there's no one here except two tied-up dogs. And then I see this stuff lying by the stove. The backpack. And some photos of horses. And some phone numbers.

"And then I see this funny newspaper clipping—a photo of the Mid-Hudson Opera Lovers Whateveryoucallit. And I'm looking at it and I see none other than Sherman Porter's ugly face in it. And I see Walter Stringfellow's face too. And another face—one that I just saw at the funeral—John Chung, Wynton's father."

Didi said, "I only recognized Stringfellow in that photo. But I never met Chung's father or this Sherman Porter. At least I don't remember meeting them."

"Probably not, Didi. Porter didn't move in your circles. Anyway, people are very funny. This old drunk Porter took all the heat Art and I could pour on and he didn't crack. But the moment he sees that photo he starts babbling. And what a tale he had to tell."

Allie lit another cigarette, walked over to Didi and sat down beside her, at her feet . . . close to the bandaged foot, which he stared at for a moment with horror.

Rose cleared her throat and said, in a much softer voice, "I can't give you a beer because I don't have any."

Allie wasn't listening. He started talking again. "The three men became friends out of a love for opera. But then the friendship became a criminal enterprise. It was lucrative and safe.

"Hard-pressed dairy farmers in the Hillsbrook area were paid cash to take care of pregnant mares until they foaled and the foal reached approximately six months of age. Then the mares and foals were vanned to area airports and flown to Hong Kong and Japan where the racing industry is booming. Accompanying the mares and their foals were fraudulent papers giving them a spectacular racing record and breeding. In fact these were the altered papers of long-dead racing mares. The people in Hong Kong had no way to know they were being fooled and they didn't really care. They needed horses that could run and virtually all U.S.-bred thoroughbreds are better than what they have. They paid big money and everybody was happy.

"Then the scheme began to unravel just a bit. Sherman Porter, one of the three in the conspiracy, decided he wanted out. So he left to go his own way with a hefty piece of change which he used for the scam that eventually landed him in prison.

"Now all this was initiated before Wynton Chung joined the Hillsbrook police force. And Wynton obviously had no idea how his father was supplementing his professional income. Interesting to note, Didi, that Wynton always complained his father didn't like his choice of profession. But it was probably that Chung Senior didn't want his son to be a cop in an area that he was using as a criminal venue.

"Chung becomes a cop. He arrests Sherman Porter and makes a good case.

"Porter tries a bluff. He tells him that if young Chung continues with the prosecution, he, Porter is going to blow the whistle on his daddy, who's a crook. Chung doesn't believe a word Porter is telling him. At least he claims not to. The case proceeds. Porter is convicted, goes to jail. He never says a word about Chung's father.

"But Porter told young Wynton enough about the horse business to make him suspicious. Just to ease his own mind he starts conducting an investigation. He finds horses hidden on dairy farms and he photographs them. He asks for part-time work from those farmers and they snap him up because the most dangerous time for them was the vanning of the horses from the barn to the airport. A police officer as a vanning security guard was like a gift. That was what the eighty-eight dollars a month was really for.

"Then Chung took his investigation one step further. He suspected Stringfellow, so he seduced his wife. Walter Stringfellow now became very worried, particularly since Chung helped Porter get out early, sent him bundles in jail and booze after he got out, and pumped him continually for more information.

"It was Willy Prosper who murdered Wynton—at Walter Stringfellow's request and for Stringfellow's money. It was the piano player who tipped them that Chung was in the restaurant. John Chung obviously had no idea his son was to be executed. He went into a deep shock.

"But the other son, Darryl Chung, did no such thing. He knew exactly what his father was doing.

He had wanted no part of it, but now he was going to seek vengeance for Wynton's death.

"He came to the funeral. He leaned on his father until he got the names of all the parties to the conspiracy. And then, without fear or favor, decided to slaughter the whole congregation in retribution.

"First, the girl who fingered his brother—Tai Draper. He murdered her while she was doing her courier route, bring the new fake pedigrees to Stringfellow.

"Next he murdered one of the farmers who kept the horses: Robert Lorenz. There were others to kill. His next one was to be one of the Bracken sisters. He came to the house. He saw an old blue Volvo parked in front. He thought it was Stringfellow's car. So he blasted away.

"He probably didn't kill you because he saw you crawl out of the car and he got confused for a moment. You obviously are not Walter Stringfellow.

"So he hesitated. And there I was. And the only reason I was there is that I realized, at least I had the suspicion, that you and Rose were up to something stupid. Otherwise you would have called me when you got the backpack from Lukacs. So we started the red Jeep through the hood—Art can do those kind of things—and Art and the cuffed Porter went to check out the Prosper place and I went to the Bracken place. And all of that stemmed from the simple fact that I took one road rather than another and spotted your Jeep. You could have been one dead beautiful veterinarian."

It was indeed a grisly tale of murderous vengeance and there was a long, somber silence in the flickering lights of the barn. Allie leaned his head against her leg, very gently. Didi let her hand rest on his head.

"Are you sure it was Prosper who killed Wynton? On Stringfellow's orders."

"No, I'm not sure. That's what Sherman Porter surmises. But to tell the truth I think that old drunk thinks he's a real shrewd character and some of it may be untrue; he figures a little lying will be to his advantage. In fact, it is Porter who is responsible for this mess. He was the one who tried to buy his way out of a conviction with some intimate family details for the arresting cop. And he was the one who kept the iron in the fire. I think Wynton visited him in Jamestown. I'd bet on it. And I think Porter kept telling Wynton just enough to keep him interested, to keep the brandy flowing when he got out."

"And what about Darryl Chung?" Rose asked.

"What about him?"

"How could he have gotten so much information so fast from his father?"

"It was probably easy. A dazed father having lost his beloved son and being questioned by another son. Poor John Chung was in this for the money. He probably never in his wildest dreams believed that his child would die because of a racing scam that shipped ponies to Hong Kong."

"Do you think"—Rose persisted—"that when

he, I mean Darryl Chung, had murdered all the players, he would have turned his weapon on his father?"

"That, thankfully, we'll never know."

"Were there other Hillsbrook people involved with the care of the mares and foals?"

"I think there were, but I don't know their names. Sherman Porter told me he heard that Fox, a man named Fox, a neighbor of Stringfellow's, was in it briefly. But he walked out after one of the foals broke loose. Fox became frightened. And that was that."

Didi nodded.

"What is it?" Allie asked.

"Nothing," she said. She was thinking of the dappled colt. That must have been the one that broke loose.

Allie stood up. "I have to get out of here. Chief Gough told me this time I should stay out of Hillsbrook until the hearing even if the town is burning down."

Art Moldava disengaged himself from the dogs and arose too.

"I don't know what to say, Doctor Nightingale. You look beautiful there, even wounded."

The two men walked out.

After their car pulled away, Rose asked, "Did you notice Officer Voegler's subtle rewriting of history?"

"No."

"Just because he arrived in time to stop you

from getting a possible bullet in the head, he now talks as if it was his investigation that broke this whole thing open. *Au contraire*. It was your investigation, girlfriend."

"I don't really care who claims credit or gets credit."

"But will he love you in the morning?"

"What does that mean, Rose?"

"Nothing. It doesn't mean a bloody thing. It's just something that popped into my head. Just like there's something I'm going to pop in my mouth now." And she went and got a bag of her number one chips—chips so arcane that the description of the contents was too small to read in the flickering light. The two friends feasted. The three dogs slavered, even though if a chip had been offered to them and they did bite into it, they would not have found it the least bit palatable.

Don't miss the next
Deidre Quinn Nightingale
mystery

**Dr. Nightingale Traps
the Missing Linx**

coming soon from Signet

It was a freezing January morning, but even so, at six a.m. Dr. Deidre Quinn Nightingale, DVM, assumed the lotus position on the cold ground. She was performing her yogic breathing exercises, watched as always at a respectful distance by the motley collection of yard dogs.

When she finished, she walked into the kitchen and joined another motley crew: the group of household retainers she had long referred to as her elves, who were just sitting down to breakfast. This appearance by the doctor at the breakfast table was most unusual. For Dr. Nightingale, Didi to her friends, never ate breakfast with the elves.

Mrs. Tunney, housekeeper and chief elf, was so surprised that she fumbled the oatmeal spoon. But old Charlie Gravis, the doctor's veterinary assistant, barely looked up, and then went back to staring gloomily into his coffee. Young Trent Tucker, general handyman and chauffeur extraordinaire, found it funny, and broke into an impish grin. And the strangely beautiful golden-haired Abigail, overseer and protector of all the on-premises animals—the yard dogs, the doctor's thoroughbred horse, and Charlie Gravis's pigs—just sat there looking as beautifically vague as ever.

Didi stirred a little brown sugar into her oatmeal. She didn't know quite how to proceed. She wanted to talk to the group about economizing, but she didn't want to alarm them. She knew that her elves did not really trust her as they had trusted her late mother, that they were afraid she would abrogate the unwritten contract that her mother had formed with them—room and board in perpetuity in exchange for basic chores dealing with house and land.

She added a little cream to her bowl and then a little more brown sugar. No one else had touched his oatmeal yet. They were all waiting for her. She had to let them know that it was crunch time. There was a cash-flow problem. January and February were always the worst months in a large animal vet's practice. But this year it seemed everything had dried up. And she had not been able to break into that closed circle of the large breeding stables. She knew she had to expand her small animal practice, but was reluctant to open the clinic more than twice a week. Meanwhile, the monthly bills mounted higher and higher. There was the medical insurance for the five of them, and the remaining payments on her Jeep, and monthly payments for the addition to the house which constituted her small animal clinic, and the taxes and the fuel bills and the loan she had taken out to pay for the last two years of vet school. And since she paid the elves no salary whatsoever, she had to purchase winter coats for them as well as clothes for herself. Then there were the skyrocketing feed bills for those pigs and for her horse, Promise Me. The weight of it all was beginning to crush her.

Didi ate, at last, a spoonful of oatmeal. Her elves followed suit.

"You want some butter for that?" Charlie asked. As he proffered the plate, the butter knife fell off with a clatter.

"Watch out for that!" Mrs. Tunney barked at him, disapproval tightening her jaw. She replaced the knife primly.

"No, thank you," Didi said.

"The toast is ready," Mrs. Tunney chirped in Didi's direction. "Rye toast this morning."

Again "No, thank you" from Didi. She ate another spoonful of oatmeal. The tension was becoming unbearable. I am ruining their breakfast, she thought.

She pushed the bowl away, stood, and announced boldly: "I just wanted to tell all of you that I'm going to the hardware store in town this morning."

The elves stared at one another, not knowing what to make of the announcement.

"Whatever you need," Didi quickly added, "make a list for me." And with that she hurried out of the kitchen, still carrying her coffee cup. *Tomorrow,* she thought as she hurried back to her room to shower and dress. I'll discuss it with them tomorrow.

Back in the kitchen, the elves resumed their breakfast.

"What do you make of it?" Mrs. Tunney asked. "Her coming in here like that."

No one replied.

"I asked a question!" Mrs. Tunney announced. "You know Miss Quinn never sits down with us at breakfast."

Charlie finally spoke up. "Guess she was hungry."

Mrs. Tunney made a face. It was obvious she considered that explanation stupid, at best. "I see dark clouds coming," she intoned.

The others continued to eat. Old lady Tunney was always seeing dark clouds coming.

"It's snowing," Charlie Gravis announced as they exited the hardware store with their bundles. It was eleven a.m.

"I am aware of the existing weather conditions," Didi said testily.

Charlie didn't speak again, but he was thinking, You should have ate your oatmeal this morning, young miss. Maybe it would've improved your mood.

"We're going to go to the diner, get some coffee, and call into the machine to see if there's any work," Didi told him.

"Sounds good," he quickly agreed. He always liked the way she spoke about veterinary work. She called it "work." Nothing fancy. Yes, he liked that about the boss.

Once at the diner they slid into a choice booth near the window. The place was half empty—between breakfast and lunch crowds.

Myra, the on-again, off-again waitress, threw the menus down without a word. Her bad manners were legendary, but no one seemed to pay her much mind. Didi went and made the call. She was back in less than a minute. "Nothing," she said simply. She and Charlie studied the menu for no reason at all, and then both ordered coffee. Charlie, on second thought, called for a toasted corn muffin, buttered, with marmalade on the side.

After Myra left to deliver the order to the kitchen, Charlie leaned over and whispered: "I hear that she has two husbands."

"Who?"

"Myra. The waitress. One in New Jersey and one in Glen Falls."

"I find that hard to believe, Charlie."

"Well, where do you think she goes when she disappears from here all the time?"

"I have no idea. But she doesn't look to me like the kind of woman who would have two husbands."

Charlie shrugged. "Anyway, if I was the owner of this diner, I'd have fired her a long time ago."

Myra brought the coffee. Two minutes later she brought the muffin. It was underdone, not nearly crisp enough, but Charlie didn't send it back.

He and Didi watched the snow as it fell. As she sat observing Charlie spread marmalade on the second half of the muffin, Didi heard: "How nice it is to finally meet you!"

She turned toward the booming male voice. Standing next to the booth was a huge fat man wearing a full-length electric blue down coat and a rather ridiculous Australian bush hat.

"I have heard of your skill as well as your beauty," the big man said. It was only at that moment that she realized he was addressing her. Charlie put the remainder of his muffin back on the plate.

"Allow me to introduce myself," the stranger continued.

Didi knew exactly who the man was; she had seen many photos of him in the local newspapers. He was Hillsbrook's latest celebrity, Buster Purchase. He had become famous as a wacky weather man at a Los Angeles television station and then made a fortune selling roomy American cars in TV ads. He had decided to retire to Hillsbrook, he told the papers, because James Cagney had retired and died in this area, and what was good enough for America's greatest tough guy actor was good enough for him.

Since moving to Hillsbrook he had become a whirlwind. The papers said he had single-handedly resurrected Hillsbrook social life. He gave parties. He raised money for charity. He started all kinds of clubs around his many hobbies, which included American Indian archaeology, the Civil War, cats, and God knew what else. Yes, Didi knew exactly who he was.

After the formal introduction the huge celebrity said, "I was wondering, Dr. Nightingale, whether you would help me with a rather serious problem."

"What problem is that, Mr. Purchase?"

"I just received word that Dr. Corcoran is snowed in at O'Hare Airport in Chicago and won't be able to get back here today. You know Dr. Corcoran?"

"I've heard of him, yes. A fine vet."

"Yes, he is. And he was supposed to be at my fundraiser today in a professional capacity. We are auctioning off some kittens at my house today. There will be excellent edibles, excellent drink, and the auction is for a very worthy cause."

"Why do you need a vet at a fund-raiser?"

"Well, these are not your ordinary kittens. And I thought it would give the fund-raiser a certain pizazz if a fine vet issued a certificate of health as each kitten is adopted after a healthy donation. You see, as I said, these are not your everyday kittens."

"What type of kittens are they?" Didi asked, now both perplexed and intrigued.

He puffed himself up and said in a rather conspiratorial voice: "*Lynx rufus rufus* Buster."

The young vet burst into laughter. Charlie transferred his look of confusion from Purchase to his young boss. Didi said to her assistant when she could control her mirth: "That is the eastern bobcat's scientific name, Charlie." Then she asked Buster Purchase, "Have you bred a new species of bobcat?"

"Not exactly, Dr. Nightingale. The daddy is a wild Michigan bobcat, and the mother is a charming Hillsbrook barn cat. The kittens, I might add, are glorious."

"Mr. Purchase, I'm sure the kittens are glorious," Didi

replied, "but I don't think you can add your name to *Lynx rufus rufus*. There are many instances of these kind of hybrids."

With a twinkle in his eye the fat man answered, "Ah, the search for immortality is a difficult one. But will you take Dr. Corcoran's place?"

"It's very short notice," Didi said, "and I think I have an appointment this evening."

"Oh it's not this evening. It's this afternoon. At four. And it'll all be over by six. I know the fee isn't that much for a vet of your caliber—only five hundred dollars but you would be helping a very worthy cause."

Didi tensed. Five hundred dollars. She didn't want to do it. But that was a princely sum for next to no work at all. She was, as her mother used to say, between the devil and the deep blue sea.

"Where is your home?" she asked. Buster Purchase beamed. He gave her precise directions, shook hands with her and with Charlie, expressed his wish that Charlie accompany her this afternoon, and rolled out of the diner.

After Purchase was gone Charlie went back to his muffin. Didi fiddled with her coffee morosely.

"You know, boss," Charlie said after a time, "I would've laid a hundred to one odds that you never would have agreed to do this—if I was a betting man, I mean."

Didi stared hard at him. She couldn't be angry with him, she realized. She hadn't told him what she was supposed to have told him and the others at breakfast.

So she smiled and said, "That's why you should never gamble, Charlie." Then she remembered that she had not asked just what Buster Purchase's worthy cause was.

Didi and her assistant arrived at the Purchase home a tad before four. She was astonished at the size of the crowd and the cross section of Hillsbrook it represented.

There were the Napiers and the Cooks—old Hillsbrook hunt people who probably hadn't been to a social event since the hounds and horses abandoned Hillsbrook.

The Mintons were there: he, a banker, she, a physician. And the Woolfs—husband and wife owners of the largest and most profitable dairy operation in the area. There was Jeremy Lukens, who owned the only men's clothing store in town and fancied himself a kind of local cultural czar. And there were a lot of people Didi knew by sight but not by name.

It was most definitely a crowd with money, but Buster Purchase had also invited the derelict poet Bert Conyers, and he was there in full regalia, including sheepskin vest and staff. Harland Frick was also in attendance. He owned the health food store in town and was Hillsbrook's oral historian.

Didi didn't see her friend Rose Vigdor. She should have just brought her along, she realized, but it was too late now.

A lovely young woman loomed up in front of them. She looked like a fashion model—willowy, pale, with chiseled features and an enormous mane of black hair.

"I'm Sissy Purchase," she announced. "You must be the fabulous Dr. Nightingale."

It has to be his wife, Didi thought, although she's young enough to be his daughter.

Sissy Purchase pulled the vet and her associate to the buffet table and left them there. It was a truly opulent spread that Didi and Charlie looked upon. Gravis dug right in. Didi, deciding to wait a few minutes before eating, walked over to Harland Frick.

"What is this party for, Harland?" she asked directly.

He polished off a stuffed cabbage before answering: "The Magruder barn."

That made sense. Didi nodded approvingly. The Magruder barn was the oldest standing one in Hillsbrook, built about 1740. And it was barely standing. The man who owned the land had died. His estate was in litigation, the barn was crumbling, and something had to be done.

"They're trying to set up a kind of watchdog committee who'll repair it, watch over it, and lobby for it until the state gives it landmark preservation status," Harland explained between bites of onion tart.

"A 'worthy cause' indeed," Didi said, feeling a little better about the whole project.

Buster Purchase then called the assembled to order.

"Children!" he bellowed. "We must proceed. The food, drink, and other frivolities will wait. This fund-raiser has commenced. The auction is afoot. All of you now please repair to the master bedroom."

"Is he joking?" Didi whispered to Harland. "How is this crowd going to fit into their bedroom?"

Frick laughed. "You haven't seen the bedroom."

They all followed instructions, moving in a wave toward the bedroom. It was indeed the largest one Didi had ever seen. Obviously when the Purchases remodeled this old farm house, they had broken through walls to make a bedroom that could hold a herd of dairy cows. It was furnished aggressively with chairs and rugs and divans and bookshelves and, in front of the gigantic four-poster, there was a sunken area that functioned as a kind of sitting room.

A glass door on the windowless side of the room signaled that the Purchases had installed a small greenhouse that one could enter from the bedroom or from without.

"Dr. Nightingale!" Buster Purchase called out. "Please take the seat of honor!" He was pointing to the bed, on which was a stack of ornate, specially printed certificates that read:

Certificate of Health
Lynx rufus rufus Buster

Two pens lay on the bed next to the certificates.

"Kinda like signing a peace treaty," Charlie noted under his breath.

Didi reluctantly sat down. She now realized she didn't like this kind of thing at all. It was nonsense. How could she give those kittens a thorough examination so quickly? It couldn't be done. It was a fake—show-biz stuff. Silently, she cursed her need for money. But it was too late to back out. She would give Purchase what he wanted—a cursory examination of each cat—eyes, ears, nose, throat, coat, conformation, muscular coordination, and other superficialities.

The fat man was in his glory. "I shall now enter the bobcat's lair," he announced gleefully, "which usually functions as our greenhouse. I'll say hello to mama cat, bring out the babies, and deliver them to good Dr. Nightingale. Upon completion of the exam, bidding will commence."

The guests applauded. Buster Purchase opened the glass door, walked into the greenhouse, and brought out six kittens, three at a time.

He placed them on the bed next to Didi, accompanied by the oohs and aahs of the crowd.

Six sets of kitten eyes looked up at her. They were truly adorable, somewhere between eight and twelve weeks old.

Four of the cats were coal black, resembling domestic kittens except that they had larger feet. The other two had bob tails, tufted ears, big feet, and black dots on charcoal gray coats.

Didi forgot her distaste for the project. She was charmed out of her boots.

But then all hell broke loose. One kitten jumped onto her shoulder. Two began chasing each other over the pillows. One headed up a post. And the remaining two started ripping up the certificates.

"Surround the bed!" Buster shouted.

A phalanx of guests complied, cordoning off possible exit routes for the kittens. A kind of order was restored.

Didi picked up one kitten at a time, examined it quickly, and signed and dated each certificate, referring to the cats as "Buster One," "Buster Two," and so on.

Then the auction commenced, with Buster Purchase serving as auctioneer. Of course, it had nothing to do with kittens and everyone knew it. It had to do with donating money to save the Magruder barn.

The two kittens who looked like their bobcat daddy went fast. One to the Napiers for $2,000. One to the Mintons for $1,600.

The rest of the litter, who resembled their barn cat mother, moved more slowly. And in the end only two were taken. One to Jeremy Lukens for $500. One to a woman Didi did not know for $360.

Then Purchase declared the fund-raiser over—it was time to do some serious eating and drinking.

"Doctor," he said, "please distribute the certificates to

the lucky parties. I shall return the two remaining kittens to their mother, who I assure you thinks they have been slighted."

Appreciative laughter all around.

Didi was astonished. Almost $5,000 raised in five minutes—in a bedroom! She handed a certificate to each of the bidders, not at all sure which cat was Buster One and which was Buster Four.

Well, what did it matter?

Buster vanished into the greenhouse with the two kittens, leaving the glass door slightly ajar.

Sissy Purchase began shepherding the guests back into the living room, including the winners who had their newly acquired bobcat hybrids and certificates in their arms.

"I can use a little help in here, Sissy," they heard Buster call.

"Be there in a second," replied his wife, busy at the moment with the poet, a bit soused, who had caught his sheepskin vest on an expensive floor lamp.

By the time she had disengaged Bert Conyers, it wasn't necessary to go to her husband's assistance. He had walked out of the greenhouse.

Someone screamed.

Buster's face and neck were lined with deep, bloody scratches.

He smiled idiotically. Then he fell forward. He was dead when he hit the ground.

Mrs. Minton rushed to him. Others ran around in a panic, searching for the phone. Sissy Purchase stood where she was, wavering, swaying on her feet as if she were about to topple over. Her hands were all tangled up in her lustrous raven hair.

Didi approached the lifeless body on the floor. Mrs. Minton was dutifully applying CPR—but to no avail.

Up close, Buster's wounds were puffy and discolored.

Didi's eyes went to the half opened door of the greenhouse. She walked quickly over to it and shut the door tightly. Then she stationed herself there like an embassy guard and listened to the sounds of a party disintegrating. She felt calm, but it was as though everything was happening in another dimension.

Only three things seemed clear.

Buster Purchase was dead.

It had to have been the mother cat who delivered the ugly scratches to the wacky weather man's face and neck.

What had entered Buster's wounds—what had killed him—had all the earmarks of rattlesnake venom.